A Slice of Life

Liron A. Galston

Published by Liron S. Ehrensperger, 2022.

A SLICE OF LIFE

First edition. August 4, 2022.

ISBN: 979-8201641504

Written by Liron A. Galston.

Table of Contents

To all who strive for happiness.

ACKNOWLEDGMENTS

This book would have stayed a pipe dream without the support and love of many people in my life.

Thank you to Susan and Lucía, for proof-reading these stories with love and care. They encouraged me to keep on writing and supported me with their friendship. I doubt this book would exist without them. I'm grateful every single day that fangirling brought us together.

Thank you also to the wonderful sensitivity readers Lenae and Callen, who granted me their time and feedback. My aim has always been to publish stories that are accurate and safe for everyone to read. Thank you for helping me to do so.

My dear friend Charlotte helped me to be brave and cheered me on through every step of my becoming, and the writing of this book. She's the best proof that good allies make us shine and support us, through thick and thin.

Last but not least my family. A big thank you to my wonderful husband Norbert. He went through so much soul-searching and several coming-outs with me, and I will be forever thankful that he supported me on my path to living as my truthful self.

Thank you also to my three children, who show me every day that living openly and unapologetically is a gift and that their lives, and those our family touches, are richer for it.

DAWN

Lukasz looks over the roofs of the still sleeping town dipped in splotches of light that cut through the darkness. The cold night air is creeping through his scrubs. He doesn't care. The goosebumps forming on his skin are a welcome distraction from the heaviness lingering in every single muscle of his body. He takes a pull on his cigarette and blows smoke rings into the dimly lit space around him. It's quiet, tranquil like he only knows it from church, when he stops by late at night to light a candle and sit with God for a while.

He rubs his eyes. He could fall asleep sitting upright here, and after giving his feet the first break in twelve hours or so, he's not sure if he can ever get them to walk again.

The door to the roof terrace opens behind him. Lukasz doesn't even turn. The warmth on his back following the noise of it falling closed is familiar and welcome. Lukasz draws a deep breath, his lungs burning with the cold air, but he can't bother to care.

Lips press against his neck, and he breathes a sigh. "Hi, babe," a deep voice rumbles deliciously into his ear.

"Hey, misiu,"* he answers, leaning back into the softness of his partner. "How was your day?"

"Long," Sean breathes and walks around Lukasz to sit down next to him. "It's finally calming down after a mess around midnight. The patients kept on ringing for us, and we were already understaffed. And you?" he asks.

"There was a bus accident at the beginning of my shift, and too many party-goers. Typical Friday night. I'm beat," Lukasz answers, taking another pull from his cigarette before passing it to Sean. He leans his head against his partner's shoulder and closes his eyes for a moment. He knows it's a dangerous game to play. He might fall asleep with Sean's scent creeping into his nostrils, intense after a night of hard work. He could bathe in it. Fuck the blood and other stains on his scrubs. He'd choose Sean over a freshly showered millionaire anytime.

He must have dozed off for a while because, when he opens his eyes again, the night has given way to orange and yellow smudging the blackish blue. He hasn't seen the sun rising in ages.

He admires God's play of colours and rubs his cheek against Sean's shoulder. "Awake, babe?" his partner asks, a smile clear in his voice. Lukasz hums. His lips twitch against the bone-deep tiredness, against gravity itself. Like this, he could sit for hours. Dipped in the light of the rising sun, tucked safely into Sean's arm, nothing can bring him down. At least, it feels like it.

"We need to pick up Lilly's birthday cake," Lukasz murmurs, the beauty of dawn mixing with reality. He has a long list of tasks waiting for him, no matter if he wants to sleep for two days straight.

"When does the party start?"

"At three." Lukasz smiles at the thought of his niece beaming at him when she sees the custom-made Ladybug cake.

"We should go home then. Catch a few hours of sleep, at least," Sean states and chuckles over the disgruntled sound leaving Lukasz's throat. "Come on, babe," he says and gets up. "Or do I need to carry you bridal-style?"

Lukasz snorts a laugh. "Not without you proposing first,"

he quips.

Sean looks at him with an unreadable gaze. He shakes his head as if to show how ridiculous the mere thought might be. The gesture doesn't match his expression, though.

Sure, they never talked about things like this, only about growing old together. No one needs a marriage certificate for that.

It shows how dog-tired Lukasz is that Sean's reaction hurts only a little. They couldn't have what Lukasz would want, anyway. His church wouldn't wed them, no matter how much his babcia** attests to what a wonderful couple the two are. Though a private ceremony could be nice, maybe with his sister as the officiant. Wioleta always had a way with words.

He pushes the thoughts away, futile as they are, and gets up from the concrete edge. He intertwines his fingers with Sean's and presses a kiss on his cheek, his lover's stubble scratching against his own.

"Home," Lukasz sighs and moves towards the staircase. But Sean is rooted to the spot, unmoving, holding him back with a firm grip on his hand. A frown graces his usually soft features. Lukasz cups his cheek. "What is it?" he whispers.

Sean's lips quirk into a lopsided smile. "If I sink onto one knee now, will you help me up again? I don't think I'd manage on my own," he chuckles.

Lukasz needs embarrassingly long to connect the dots. He smiles softly at his partner and brushes his lips over Sean's. "Yes," he breathes. Maybe it's an answer to the request or the question Sean might ask.

It doesn't matter. They melt into each other, exhaustion mingling with twilight. It feels surreal and magical all at once.

They hold each other for a long moment until even their joint strengths can't keep them up any longer.

"Come, misiu. Our bed is calling," Lukasz whispers as if it were a secret. Sean chuckles, the sound vibrating into Lukasz's chest and wrapping warmly around his heart. Yes, this man, he would marry, no questions asked. Maybe he will ask him seriously one day, or this was it, the voicing of intent. Lukasz is too tired to analyse it right now. He has a lifetime to figure it out, he supposes. Many more dawns for sure.

*misiu = Polish for 'teddy bear'**babcia = Polish for 'grandma'

A DAY OUT

Nicole pedals a little harder. It shouldn't be that difficult to keep up with a runner while riding a bike, but she's a bit out of practice, to put it mildly. Why did she have to fall in love with a passionate triathlete? Not that she would complain. Melissa is one of the smartest and most incredible women she's ever met. And she's beautiful, inside and out. That she can best her like this is frankly embarrassing. Melissa doesn't seem to mind, though. Maybe she's simply too concentrated on mastering this uphill run to give much thought to her barely keeping up girlfriend. Or she's kind enough not to tease, which is more likely. Melissa's kindness had struck Nicole first when they met.

The way she had cared for the crowd of people cramming her small dorm room on an impromptu advent event. She had offered tea and read a story from a friend's newly published book. It had been beautifully illustrated, but Nicole only had eyes for her. She didn't even know her name back then. Her mutual friend Kylie had dragged her there, saying it was such a nice evening thing and that Melissa wouldn't mind having a stranger there.

Nicole still remembers the butterflies storming her stomach, looking at Melissa from her spot in the dark entrance, Melissa's voice washing warmly over her as her orange tea warmed Nicole's insides. Sometimes, Melissa smiled at her warmly from her place on the bed, though there was a tall stranger always at her side, leaning into her in an intimate way that Nicole had only ever shared with her ex-boyfriend Marc. Melissa had caught her off-guard, made her forget about uni and her fears of failing for as long as the get-together lasted. Nicole returned to every single reading from then on, sad when they stopped with the winter break.

"What are you thinking about?" Melissa asks, stopping to wait for Nicole to catch up. How could she fall behind with gearing and all?

"The winter ball," Nicole pants. "Oh. You were so beautiful."

Melissa smiles at the memory of their first dance together. "Not as beautiful as you."

"I disagree, but I don't have enough air in my lungs to elaborate."

Melissa throws her head back, laughing. It's pure mirth, no condescension, no laughing *at* her. Nicole will never understand how a person so disciplined with her own body doesn't fall into the trap of feeling superior over others' less perfect ones, how she still finds beauty in them, especially Nicole's.

"This is a rough route, Niki. Sorry, I was just so thrilled that you asked to join me. I hate being away from you for so many hours for the training," Melissa says and presses a kiss to Nicole's lips. It tastes like salted caramel, Nicole's favourite ice cream flavour.

"It's okay, Lissa. I know how much the competition means to you."

Melissa looks at her for a long moment with an unreadable look on her face. "Not more than you. You know that, right?" she asks.

Nicole gapes at her. Where the hell did that come from? Insecure Melissa is such a rare sight, it always takes Nicole off-guard whenever she comes to light.

"Of course, what...?"

Melissa shakes her head, her eyes lingering somewhere on the top of the hill.

"Lis, what's wrong?"

"Ah, nothing."

Nicole breathes a sigh and lets it go. Her girlfriend will tell her when she's ready.

"Let's walk the rest," Melissa says.

"I can manage," Nicole replies.

"I know, Niki. I just want to enjoy the view with you. Lock up your bike to that tree."

"But your training..."

"I'm well ahead of schedule. I have time to take a walk with my girlfriend."

Who is Nicole to protest such a sweet offer? She does as told, then brushes the sweat off her forehead. She wipes her hands on her equally damp shirt and offers one to Melissa, who slots her fingers eagerly with hers.

"This is my favourite panorama route," she says as they slowly make their way further up the hill. "The forest on top is a great bonus once you've made it up there, especially on warm days like today." She falls silent for a long moment. "I often jogged with my father here."

"You jogged with him?" Nicole doesn't know much about Melissa's parents, has never met them, and she's not one to pry.

"He made me do all kinds of sports, signed me up for my first half-triathlon. It was so much fun. He was so proud when I came in fifth. I was disappointed, of course. You know how competitive I am." Nicole chuckles. She sure does. And if there is one bad trait about her girlfriend, then it's that she's a sore loser.

"I'm sure it made you train only harder."

"It sure did. The next time I came in second, and then I held the first for four consecutive years until I grew out of my age bracket. But I won't bore you with that."

"You never bore me. I'm the same with my music. Not as competitive. I just want this for myself."

"You never wanted to compete or play in a better band?"

Nicole snorts a laugh. She knows her indie whatever-flows-their-boat-right-now rock band isn't exactly Melissa's cup of tea. She still comes to every gig they manage to get and cheers the loudest when Nicole plays a bass solo.

"I like playing with people I vibe with, but I also enjoy polishing my technique, or practising a line to a song I'll never play with anyone but to a playback."

Melissa smiles at that and squeezes her hand. Nicole wonders if she thinks she's silly, but she doesn't dare ask. Most days, she still can't fathom that Melissa wants to be with her. Her! Someone who can't run a mile without getting a stitch. She, who still can't swim and whose endurance doesn't even get her up this stupid mountain.

"Pretty boring, huh?" she can't help asking.

"It shows how much you love your instrument. I think it's admirable. I mean, even without competitions, I'd do sports, but I'm not sure if I'd enjoy it as much. I always need a big goal. I need outside validation while you are happy with reaching a goal for yourself. I'm pretty sure your mindset is healthier than mine."

Now it's Nicole's turn to squeeze her girlfriend's hand.

"This isn't a competition, Lissa. We're all different. And that's a good thing, don't you think?"

Melissa stops still in her tracks and turns to her. "You're right. I couldn't be with a doppelgänger of mine. I need you to balance me out."

Nicole gapes at her. She wasn't aware that Melissa saw it that way. The thought spreads warmly through her chest. God, she's so in love with this woman.

They climb the hill mostly in silence, the smell of the woods and birdsongs filling the air between them. They nod to the people they meet on the way up, a few doing sports, some simply taking a walk.

"Are those lesbians?" a little kid about five stage-whispers to their mother. The woman turns crimson.

"Probably," she says. "They could be bi, too, or pan."

The couple chuckles. "One each," Melissa calls over.

"Cool!" the kid calls back and gives them a thumbs up.

"I must agree," Nicole says. "We're pretty cool."

Melissa smiles. "That we are, Niki," she says and presses a gentle kiss to her girlfriend's lips. She tugs on her hand. "Come. Only a few more metres, and I'll show you my favourite place in the world."

Nicole follows easily. And a few minutes later, standing in Melissa's arms, her breath fanning out over her neck as she points out landmarks in the valley spreading below them, Nicole must agree. This is her favourite place, too.

GOOD OLD SATURDAYS

Gabriel sits up on the side of their bed and brushes the sleep out of his eyes. "Alex?" he asks quietly. Alexander, his partner of 52 years, doesn't make a sound, but Gabriel still knows he's awake. It's one of *those* days it seems.

He slips into his house shoes, puts his glasses on, and wraps himself into the bathrobe that Alexander got for him last Christmas. It's warm and fluffy. The colour brings out the green of his eyes, Alexander always says. He's still a charmer like that. And it still works on Gabriel. Probably because Alexander is the most sincere person he's ever met in his long life.

Gabriel walks into the kitchen and fills the coffee machine, watching the life-giving liquid fill the glass pot drop by drop. He should have stayed in bed, cuddling his man, but his legs are restless, and he's always been a nervous type, barely sitting still for a moment. Sometimes, he wonders how Alexander has put up with him for so long. His beloved is quite the opposite. Alexander has always loved hours spent on the couch, lost in a book, or taking baths that leave his skin even more wrinkly than it already is. Those things would drive Gabriel up the wall, but he loves the calmness that flows out of his partner. Even his restless soul isn't immune against his steady nudging to relax and indulge.

Dotty, their elderly cocker spaniel joins him in the kitchen, pressing her head against his pyjama clad leg. After a thorough ruffle of her fur, she follows him to the front door. He picks her up and carries her down the two flights of stairs for her morning pee in front of the apartment block. He waves at

Penny from the bakery next door while he waits for Dotty to finish her business.

On his way in he takes his magazine out of the letterbox as he's done every single Saturday since they moved into this flat three decades ago. Thirty years. Time flies by when you're happy.

He carries Dotty back upstairs and chuckles when he lets her down again, huffing a little. "I'm not getting any younger, huh?" he asks. His dog looks at him with warm eyes and wags her tail. He pats her on the head and grabs his magazine.

Back in the kitchen, Gabriel fills two mugs with coffee, puts two teaspoons of sugar in Alexander's thermos one and a proper splash of milk in his own rainbow unicorn cup that his grand-niece got him two birthdays ago. Then he returns to their bedroom, Dotty trotting right after him and making herself comfortable on the soft dog bed set aside for her in the corner.

"Can you move?" Gabriel asks as he puts Alexander's mug on the bedside table.

"Give me another hour," Alexander chuckles and stretches a little, but Gabriel can see the strain on his face.

"Don't force yourself, love," he says and leans down to press a gentle kiss on Alexander's cheek. His partner sighs.

"Can you let some light in?" he asks.

"Sure," Gabriel replies and pulls the heavy curtains away. Sunlight floods the room. Alexander squints against the onslaught of brightness.

"You're blindingly beautiful," he says. Gabriel laughs.

"You silly man."

"You love me for it," Alexander smirks.

"That I do."

Gabriel walks around their bed and sits down against the headboard, propping up the magazine on his knees, one hand going to his coffee mug, the other to Alexander's back, brushing gently up and down. His partner relaxes under his touch. He can't do much to ease his pain, but he can do this. It's a routine, easy and familiar as breathing. Touch has always been their way to connect, neither of them big talkers.

Gabriel is halfway through his magazine and long out of coffee when Alexander finally makes it into an upright position after a long journey of easing his stiff joints into movement.

"Is the coffee still warm?" Gabriel asks.

"Yes, babe. As always," Alexander says and winks at him. It's a bit strained, but it still makes Gabriel's heart stutter. Alexander takes Gabriel's hand and squeezes it. His partner ignores the tremor in Alexander's hand. It's as much a part of him as his brown eyes, the scar on his right eyebrow from when he had chickenpox as a child, or the tattoo on his chest—a heart with their initials. He got it during his army time, far away from home, not knowing if he'd ever make it back. He couldn't tell his fellow soldiers about Gabriel waiting at home for him. He probably told them a female name when he asked them to scribe the GF into his skin. But it kept him focused on surviving, just like the lock of Gabriel's then sprouting hair hidden in silk paper, a lucky charm of sorts. It still lies in the top drawer next to his good shirts.

Gabriel runs his hand over his long balding head. Who would have thought that Alexander would be the one to sport a head of full white hair in old age? Gabriel chuckles at the irony.

"What?" Alexander asks, irritated by the sound.

"Ah, nothing. Just a memory," Gabriel says and puts his hand over Alexander's heart, right over the tattoo hidden under his nightshirt. Alexander smiles in understanding.

"You made me pull through," he remembers. "I hated every day being apart from you."

"I aged at least a decade while you were gone," Gabriel says. "Probably lost all my hair because of that."

Alexander chuckles. "Yes. Most definitely not your father's genes that are responsible for that," he quips. Gabriel snickers.

"Fiona still has her full magnificent head of hair. And she missed Jerry at least as much," Alexander ponders. "We should invite them for brunch. It's been way too long since we last saw each other."

"She got her hip replacement a few weeks ago," Gabriel says. "I'll call and ask if she can climb all the stairs up here."

Alexander nods and breathes a sigh. "I wish I could go for a walk with you and Dotty. I miss that." The cocker spaniel pricks up her ears and walks to Alexander's side of the bed. He lets his hand fall on her head, looking at her with sad eyes. She presses into the touch and nudges him to ruffle her fur. He obliges just too willingly.

"I could ask the boys from the shared flat if they'd come over to carry you downstairs," Gabriel offers. Alexander shakes his head.

"That's too much effort for a little walk, sweetheart. Who knows how far I'll even get."

"I'd carry a chair for you to rest in between. It would be worth every step and every ray of sunshine falling on your pretty face," Gabriel says. Alexander chuckles at that.

"You're way too charming."

"Only for you."

It's not exactly the truth. Gabriel has always loved to flirt with everyone who was happy about it from the meat seller at their local market to the sweet mother of five living on the first floor. It's in his very nature, but for half a century, the only one he really had eyes for has been his Alex.

"I never thought we'd get so far," he muses. Alexander raises a questioning eyebrow. "I never thought we'd become so old," Gabriel adds in lieu of an explanation. Alexander hums.

"But we're still here. Maybe not rocking anymore but definitely rolling," he says, glancing at his wheeled walker.

"Yeah," Gabriel smirks. "And I love every minute of it."

Alexander huffs a mirthless laugh. "You never want things to be different?" he asks, eyes vulnerable. Gabriel knows his partner thinks he's a burden, not able to leave the house, sometimes not even the bed. But that's not how Gabriel sees it. He loves caring for his love, who's been his rock and still is. One doesn't need physical strength and health to be a pillar for the people around them. Besides, he knows Alexander would do just the same if their roles were reversed.

"Of course, I wish you could be in better health, that you'd still be strong on your feet. I wish we could still walk in the park and bicker about which birds we're hearing or if the mushrooms we found were safe to eat. But apart from that? No. I've got everything I need, and then some," he says.

Alexander takes his hand, squeezing it with all the strength he can muster with his gout-ridden hands. Gabriel moves it to his lips and presses a gentle kiss on its back.

"I'd love to be in my twenties again," Alexander muses. "Wouldn't you?"

Gabriel chuckles. "We were pretty stupid at that time."

"Speak for yourself," Alexander teases. "Also, you were smart enough to kiss me, weren't you?"

"Touché," Gabriel chuckles.

They fall silent after that for a while, Gabriel resting his head on his partner's shoulder.

"You're right," Alexander whispers into the easy quiet, brushing his hand over the soft fabric of Gabriel's bathrobe.

"About what?"

"I love every minute with you, too."

NIGHT RIDE

Clara doesn't remember when exactly she fell in love with her colleague Willow. It feels like it's always been there. At least, ever since she pulled her out of the line of fire when she had frozen during her very first operation and had held her through the aftershocks. But she also knows that this isn't quite true. Back then, she wasn't even aware that she was capable of falling for another woman. She wasn't interested in women that way. Not in anyone, really. Or so she thought. That's something Willow taught her without even knowing. It simply happened.

First, it had felt foreign, like something that didn't belong to her, something that shouldn't exist. While others had started dating in their teens, Clara had studied for the best grades, hung out with her friends, and played bass in a punk band. She didn't need a partner. She didn't even want one. When she said that, people told her that she simply hadn't found the right person yet. God, how much she had hated that saying.

It was kinda true, though. That bugged her for some time, but she's over that now. It is what it is.

Is it normal to always have this fuzzy feeling in your stomach whenever your crush smiles at you? Is it usual that the mere thought of your special someone dying rips you into a million pieces?

Maybe.

Not that Clara could ask anybody about it. Willow not only taught her how to feel, but also that talking about feelings isn't cool. She always makes jokes about it, but maybe it's simply to fit in with the guys. It's hard enough to survive as a woman in this field. It's easier to assimilate than to risk showing who you really are.

Clara knows Willow better, though. She's seen her soft side, the woman who cares too much for her own sake, who cries in her car and likely alone in her flat, but never in front of others, Clara the only exception to this iron rule.

Willow is full of feelings, a far cry from her image of a tough woman who doesn't give a shit about anything but work. She's so full of them that Clara sometimes wonders if a person can choke on them. Many of them are good, some bad. Clara knows that Willow hides many things under a facade of cockiness and nonchalance. But it's only that. A facade. Willow may be the most emotional human who has ever walked the earth. The most loving sister, daughter, and friend. She doesn't need to talk about how deeply she experiences the claviature of feelings, may it be love, hate, fear, or joy. It's in every move she makes, in every word she says, in every decision she arrives at. At least, for Clara, it's as clear as day.

Willow isn't perfect and yet, she is in Clara's eyes. Because she is allowed to see her in rare fragile moments, baring her very soul. Willow is beautiful in so many ways, from her strong body over her kind eyes to her gentle soul. Clara would fight to the very last tendril of her strength if it meant to be near Willow and to keep her safe.

Clara looks at Matt's hair in front of her. It's seldom enough that Willow lets the younger detective ride her car. But Willow is dead tired from a long month of chasing leads. So tired that she has let her guard down.

It's a rare occasion, and Clara cherishes it. The blue-tinted night, the car's rumbling engine, and Willow's head lying on her shoulder.

Clara hasn't moved for miles. Why would she? Willow's head is the sweetest weight. And Willow is so close.

Awake, Willow would never let herself go like this. Clara knows. But that her subconscious lets Willow do that in her vulnerable state makes Clara incredibly happy. Willow trusts her. Despite her shortcomings, despite the mistakes she has made, for all her faults.

Clara smiles. She's content, and the night is calm. Matt is driving and for once, there is no murderer needing to be found. Maybe that'll change tomorrow, but she doesn't think about that now. She relishes Willow's body leaning into her side, her cheek brushing against the collar of her blouse, and the soft caress of her breath on the skin of her neck. She savours the quiet snores, Willow's hand that ended up between their thighs, their bumping knees and Willow's scent, intoxicating in a way no human being was ever meant to experience.

It's just a journey through the night but so much more in the grand scheme of things. It's possibly the closest Willow will ever be to her. And that's alright. Clara has made her peace with it a long time ago. This is enough. Has to be enough. And still...

Clara looks into the rear-view mirror, meets Matt's gentle eyes there. Her colleague quirks a smile, and Clara returns it. Does Matt know? Maybe.

Matt looks back at the road again, and Clara can't stop herself from pressing a soft kiss into Willow's hair. This woman deserves all the love, all the tenderness, even though she likes to brush it off as sentimental and inappropriate.

Clara doesn't care. She's in love, and her beloved is close and safe next to her. That's all she needs.

The detective looks out of the window and up to the night sky. As a girl, she watched the stars every night from her bedroom window, learnt everything about them coming into existence and still, their light was never as radiant as Willow's soul, never as burning as Clara's love, and never as steady as the amicable bond between them.

There are things that Clara doesn't allow herself to do in everyday life. She would never cross the line that separates friends from lovers. Because Willow isn't ready for that, maybe never will be. And that's okay.

She takes whatever Willow gives her freely. Brushing hands because they always stand too close, crooked smiles, long looks, and reluctant hugs. It's enough. For Clara, Willow and everything that makes her *her*, will always be enough.

And so she leans her head on Willow's as they drive through the night, raindrops painting gentle patterns on the windows. And Clara is content. Her blood sings like creation itself. It's peaceful and calm, soulful and warm. It's loving Willow, how she lets herself be loved and seeing this love reflected, not in words, but in looks and gestures.

Clara is happy. Willow is safe. Not in her arms. But close enough.

MOVING IN

"I tell you," Dennis pants. "If you weren't so damn sexy in this tank top, I wouldn't do this."

He leans against the staircase wall and brushes the back of his hand over his forehead, trying his best to keep the sweat away from his eyes.

Raheem chuckles.

"I love you, too."

Dennis rolls his eyes.

"Hey, princesses! Move your chit-chat to the next floor," Caelan calls up from the flight below. "This bed is heavy as shit."

"God, I'm so happy that you left the living room furniture at your old place," Dennis sighs.

"Come on. Only one storey left. Ready?"

"Yes, Rah, I'm ready," Dennis groans. "But you owe me the best damn blow job of all time because I won't be able to move tonight," he adds.

"I heard that," Caelan calls, faux disgust lacing xyr voice. Noa, Dennis' ex and best friend, snickers loudly. Raheem's already flushed face grows impossibly redder.

"I take it back," he says to his boyfriend. "I hate you."

Dennis chuckles and grabs the shelf.

"Hate sex is one of the best I've ever had, so…" He smirks.

"Yes, I definitely hate you," Raheem says and presses a kiss to Dennis' lips.

It had been his stupid idea to do the moving all on their own, despite having the money to pay professional movers. But something about doing this old-school, with sweat and swears and loads of pizza afterwards spoke to him. If everything goes well, this will be the last time he'll be moving in his life. He wants to savour it.

Three years of a long-distance relationship lie behind them, then a six-month intermezzo in which Raheem had moved into a shared flat with Caelan a few streets over. A stupid decision in hindsight. He'd basically lived in Dennis' flat ever since, only returning to his home to wash his clothes and pick up stuff he needed.

But he'd wanted to do this right, to give them the option of separating if everyday life turned out to be not as peachy as the longing and thrill the distance had granted them with.

He shouldn't have worried, though. Dennis is the man of his dreams. Smart, beautiful, funny—the whole package. Still, it's a big step for him, for both of them, and he wants to cherish the moment, wants to feel it in his bones that he's not a guest anymore, but someone to stay with.

Raheem has lived in many places, moved around the world, sometimes because he didn't have a choice, sometimes because he wanted to. But he doesn't feel like ever leaving this place again. For the first time in his life, he is at home somewhere. It's not just sunshine and roses, of course, but he has friends who accept him the way he is, a boyfriend who loves him, a good job, and—most importantly—a sense of belonging.

Raheem grabs the bottom of the shelves they rested on the landing and winks at Dennis, nods his head to make him tilt the furniture again. It's a tight fit around the narrow corners of the staircase, and there's no way to disassemble the artisan woodwork, but they don't give up. They manoeuvre it back and forth and carry it up way too many steps—96 in total to be precise—until they finally reach the front door of their flat.

Their.

The word still sounds strange, sends butterflies through Raheem's stomach.

It feels like something is clicking into place when his shelves end up in their study, next to Dennis' old Billy bookcases. Raheem's grandfather had built it many decades ago, finest craftsmanship in the tradition of his homeland, with intricate carvings in dark-stained wood. Raheem will have to fix some of the notches that appeared today despite their best efforts, but it's not the first time he will put the time and love into what represents his roots just as much as his future.

"My old furniture looks like garbage next to yours," Dennis says.

"But it's functional," Raheem points out, secretly agreeing.

Dennis wipes off his sweaty hands on his shirt and chuckles.

"And doesn't that sum up our personalities?" he smirks.

Raheem furrows his brow. "What do you mean, Dee?"

His boyfriend shrugs.

"You're artistic, looking for beauty in the strangest places. And I'm more practical, boring, maybe," Dennis says and runs his hand over his neck in a nervous gesture. Raheem finds it endearing but it also makes his heart clench whenever he sees it.

He pulls Dennis into his arms, presses a kiss on his lips, and nudges his nose against his boyfriend's.

"A—You're anything but boring. And B—Opposites attract."

Dennis huffs a half-hearted laugh and kisses him back.

"Hey, no smooching until everything is up here," Noa calls from the doorway.

"Yes, ma'am," Dennis chuckles.

"You only want the pizza. That's all you came for. Be honest," Caelan says, popping up behind her. Xe tickles her sides until she squirms.

"I would never..." she protests, trying her best to get away from xem.

"Caelan is right," Dennis laughs. "I know you only do it for food."

"I can buy my own pizza," Noa tries again, doing her best to keep a straight face, but failing miserably before she bursts out in laughter.

"Sure you can," Raheem says. "But well-earned, it will taste even better."

"So true," Dennis says. "It's only the dresser and the coffee table, right?" Raheem nods. "Let's put in the order and the pizza should be here when we're done."

Raheem ducks his head to conceal the smile blooming on his face. Yes, Dennis is the organised force to his creative chaos, the planner to his impulse-driven soul.

How many times did Raheem forget to eat when being in a creating storm? How many times did he miss paying a bill or didn't appear at a meeting? He hasn't missed a single meal since they've been factually living together. And Dennis hasn't gotten lost in the depths of his do-to lists ever since either. They're good for each other. Really good.

Raheem still thinks that while Dennis curses like a sailor when he crushes his toes because his sweaty hands slip and the dresser free-falls on his foot. He still thinks it when he burns his mouth with the triple cheese pizza, and when they wash off the grime of the day under a joint shower, his attempt of saying thank you in a more palpable way cruelly disrupted by the slippery shower tub.

It doesn't matter.

They giggle like teenagers as Raheem sits on his butt, looking up at the man he loves. He'll regret his decision to do the moving on their own in the morning, his muscles already burning with a vengeance. But he'll never regret the decision to make a move on the gorgeous stranger sitting at the hotel bar, to exchange numbers after a conversation about all and sundry, and all the many small and big steps that brought him to this moment, sitting laughing under the spray in their shower with his tailbone hurting like hell.

He presses a kiss to Dennis' knee and waits until his partner is on solid ground to help him up. He slips once more and falls into Dennis' arms with a surprised wince. Dennis catches him and leans his forehead against his boyfriend's, laughing the tension out of his body.

"Anaa ba'hibbak, habeebee,"[*] Raheem whispers and leans into Dennis' body.

"Not hating me any longer, honey?" Dennis teases.

Raheem sticks out his tongue and pulls back to rub himself dry.

"I love you, too," Dennis says. "Even when you make me carry furniture four flights up."

Raheem grins at him. 'Yes,' he thinks. 'Best move ever.'

*Anaa ba'hibbak, habeebee = Arabic for 'I love you, my darling.'

COMING HOME

It's late. Just another of those days, and Janina hates it. Hates that the light in Danelle's room is still shining as it always does when Janina pulls a late-nighter. It warms her heart, but she can't help feeling bad about it. She did send her partner a text about the missing kid, though. Not that she expected Danelle to go to bed knowing how much this case would unsettle her. But one can hope.

Danelle surely had a long day, too. She may work only part-time now since moving to Riverside, but their teenage daughters can be a handful. Her job at the sweet shop keeps Danelle on her feet all day long, three times a week. Then the household chores, all that boring everyday stuff that used to eat Janina up from the inside, back when she was freshly widowed and a full-time working single parent.

Her husband Jack used to wait for her like this, too, often with little Susie snuggled against his chest. The smile he always gave her to take away the guilty conscience was way different from the one she knows awaits her behind Danelle's door. The door that stands ajar as always when her shift or an urgent case keeps her from coming home at a more socially acceptable hour. It's a silent invite that Janina appreciates very much today. She sticks her head through the gap and gives her partner a tired wave of her hand. Danelle grins widely at her, beaming like only she can at half past one in the morning.

"Hiya. How was your day, dear?"

Janina is good at holding herself together. So damn good. But she kept it up for hours of searching, dealing with the crime scene, and the press conference. Now, she crumbles in front of her partner, who surely deserves sleep instead of a messy pile of sheriff on her doorstep.

Danelle's grin morphs into an empathetic, soft smile. She gets up and walks over to Janina, who is still rooted to the spot, shoulders slumped and head tipped back. She really doesn't want to cry now, but the tears prick her eyes with a fiery force.

"Oh, Jan. Come here," Danelle says with all the tenderness that her partner craves so much. She hugs her and pulls her face to the crook of her neck. Janina melts into the embrace, leans some of the weight of the past day against the sturdy, soft presence of the woman who has become her home, so much more than the walls of this house that have seen so much loss and pain.

The girls had brought life and purpose beyond her job, but Danelle brought light. Not the tender light of romantic love all fuzzy and rosy. Not the harsh light of blood family that often hurts in their judgement and their tendency to open nearly healed wounds. Not the comforting light of friendship that shines on you from time to time. No.

Danelle's light warms Janina from the inside, makes her roll her eyes, huff a laugh, sigh with relief, and breathe so much easier.

Janina's tears wet Danelle's pyjama top, and it feels so good to let go. Danelle holds her with the strength of a woman who has seen the ugly side of the world and who still manages to see the good, even in hopeless situations. Danelle holds her with the love of someone who gets her, without explanations or expectations. She holds her with the reverence of someone who likes to cover up her own pain but would never do the same with someone else's.

And Janina loves her for all of this, for being allowed to come home at night, shoes still covered in mud from the search, sad and defeated, empty and oh-so tired.

"Wanna sleep in my bed tonight?" Danelle asks, and Janina just nods against her shoulder. "Need some help?" The answering silence makes Danelle pull back. She beholds her partner, cups Janina's cheek tenderly, feeling her leaning into it as her eyes close shut in exhaustion. Danelle nods in understanding, and Janina accepts the tender kiss against her temple before Danelle opens her belt and undresses her until she's left standing in her underwear.

Danelle is affectionate, always, with everybody she loves. And they've come a long way from that first meeting at a retreat for single mothers to this very day, where Janina allows her to touch her like this without a second thought. It's nothing sexual. Janina never needed that part, not even back with Jack, and Danelle doesn't care about it anymore. Not after husband number two. Maybe she never really did in the first place. But she cares about Janina and their girls, the family they created out of love, not only based on blood.

Janina slips into one of Danelle's shirts, sinks into her partner's arms, and wraps herself around her like she does not often allow herself to do. Like that, the events of the day start settling, and it takes a long while until Janina's sobs subside, until Danelle switches off the light, and they both fall asleep.

The next morning, Janina wakes up alone in Danelle's bed. The voices of Susan and Anna are coming subdued from the kitchen, and the telltale sound and smell of eggs and bacon frying in a pan reach Janina's senses together with the soft humming of a melody. She loves that sound so much because it means that Danelle is relaxed and well-rested. Janina smiles to herself and takes a deep breath before she gets up.

"Good morning, girls," she greets as she walks into the kitchen, still tying up her dressing gown. Her daughters mumble a tired 'morning' back.

"Did you sleep well, dear?" Danelle asks with a soft smile, tender eyes scanning Janina's face.

"Like a log. Thank you." Danelle nods knowingly and presses a mug with hot coffee into her hand. She takes a sip and sighs. "Are you up for a walk after breakfast, sweetheart?" Janina asks.

Danelle's smile widens, and she squeezes Janina's hand lying on the worktop. "You betcha!"

PINS AND NEEDLES

Blair unclenches their hand slowly. They wince at the pins and needles torturing it. How the hell did they manage to have their arm falling asleep in this cloud of a bed. *Oh, right.*

They smile at the sweet heat creeping from behind into their skin. *Noah.* God, they never thought they might land this beautiful man, but they somehow did. The memories of last night are still a little fuzzy in their sleep-clouded mind, but what they do remember was hot, and sweet, and the best sex they'd had in a very long time.

Blair lets their fingers dance through the air, trying their best not to wake the man wrapped around their body while waking up their sleeping limb. It only half-works as Noah starts stirring behind them. So Blair rolls around slowly to look at him when he opens his eyes.

Noah's lips wake up first, a smile tugging on their corners. Butterflies storm through Blair's stomach. They could get used to starting their day like this, wrapped up in warmth and to a gentle smile that makes them feel like their chest might explode with affection.

"Mornin'," Noah murmurs. "Sleep well?"

"Perfect," Blair whispers, the moment too intimate to speak at moderate volume. "Your mattress is..."

"Awesome, isn't it? Since I bought it, I'm spending way more time in bed." Noah chuckles.

Blair smirks at him and places a peck on the tip of Noah's nose. They consider their conquest for a moment. They've known about each other for a while, ran into each other at mutual friends' places, but only yesterday, they properly talked for the first time and the whole world fell away, as if it was only the two of them in a noisy room full of people.

Blair is used to one-night stands, but they aren't sure if this is one, if Noah wants it to be one. The uncertainty makes them feel off-kilter. But Noah smiles shyly, a blush creeping into his cheeks and Blair realises that he is just as insecure about this as they are.

Last night was so easy. Maybe it was the dimmed light, the frenzy of passion, and Noah's voice whispering silly things into their ear. They both had no booze, so this was at least not a quickie induced by it. They took a cab to Noah's place. They made it to the bedroom. Neither of them should regret this happening, which is strangely comforting, because Blair doesn't want Noah to regret it. They want this to be a start and not just a single event in time, and isn't that something?

That's new. Blair likes being vocal about independence and their fight against heteronormativity and the silliness of monogamy. Noah agreed last night on the balcony at their friend's place. He agreed, and Blair needs to hide their face on Noah's shoulder so as not to let him see the worry on it. Maybe he hooked up with them because of it. Maybe he thought they were just someone to have fun with for one night.

Blair doesn't even know why they care. They aren't into committed relationships, but something about this man makes them question everything. *Damn!* Their friend Matt had warned them that this would happen one day. They had laughed into his face, and now here they are, in the bed of a practical stranger, and Cupid's arrow, still sticking in their chest, has wounded them hard. But it's nice, too—the butterflies, the excitement, even the worry. They just hope it's all worth it.

"Regrets?" Noah asks, his voice cautiously schooled.

Blair pulls back, considers him for a long moment. "No. None. You?"

Noah quirks a lopsided smile and shakes his head.

"Good," Blair croaks, a flood of emotions tightening their throat. "Do you have coffee?"

Noah screws up his face. "I'm a tea drinker, sorry. But there's a coffee shop around the corner," he says and jumps out of bed, fishing for his boxers and jeans. Before Blair can protest, he slips into his jumper and smiles at them. "Which one shall I get you?"

Blair gapes at him for a long moment. He's planning to pick it up and have them drink it with him in his flat. The coffee shop thing isn't an excuse to get them out of his home. A smile blooms on their face.

"Black as my soul," they smirk.

Noah snorts. "You sure I shouldn't bring you a sweet concoction with rainbow sprinkles, because I think that suits your soul way better," he jokes.

Blair snickers. "Nah, black is just fine."

"Back in a minute," Noah says and presses a long-lingering kiss to their lips. "Take what you need. Bathroom's at the end of the hallway. Towels are in the cabinet." And with that, he disappears through the door.

Blair closes their eyes and slowly lets out a breath. They're glad to have a moment for themself to sort through their feelings.

Noah is nice, funny, silly, smart, has a good job, a freehold flat, and a wicked tongue. He's perfect boyfriend material, basically everything Blair usually *doesn't* want. But here, lying in his cloudy bed, with Yoda above his bed and Funko Pops staring at them from the other side of the room, Blair can't help but think it would be nice to have something serious for once. They just don't know if Noah thinks the same.

Blair breathes a sigh. They throw back the blanket and shuffle to the bathroom. Maybe a shower will clear their mind.

A few minutes later, they walk into the kitchen, hair still wet and smelling like Noah's shampoo. The man of the house is already busy preparing breakfast.

"You're not vegan, are you?"

Blair shakes their head. "Used to be, but eggs are fine," they say and take a slice of bread out of the toaster, nibbling on it while watching Noah make an omelette.

"I saw the cross-stitch hanging in the corridor," they cut through the silence. It wasn't exactly uncomfortable, but they feel like they should fill it. "That yours?"

Noah hums. "Yeah, it's a hobby of mine." He smiles shyly, and Blair's insides melt a little at the sight of it.

"My grannie used to do it when I was a child. She always pushed the needle through the fabric and I was allowed to pull it through. But that was thicker," they say.

"There are different forms of embroidery. I prefer cross-stitch. It's systematic and relaxes me."

"Didn't know there were patterns for nerdy stuff."

Noah chuckles. "There are patterns for *everything*. But I created some of them myself."

"Really? That's awesome."

"You don't think it's ridiculous?"

Blair makes an affronted face. "No! Why would I?"

Noah shrugs. "My ex found it stupid."

"The only thing stupid was your ex."

Noah huffs a mirthless laugh. "You might be right. But he's history, so... Your coffee's getting cold."

"Oh, right," Blair says and grabs the paper cup. The drink is still burning hot. They blow over it as they watch Noah throwing together a breakfast, suitable for monarchs, with ease. Okay, maybe Blair exaggerates a tiny bit in their mind, but the table fills with more food than their fridge holds, and they wonder briefly if Noah does this for all of his *guests*, then if he has many *guests* over. They stop this train of thought and slump in one of the chairs.

"Any plans for today?" they ask.

"Depends," Noah replies with his back to them.

"On what?" Blair can see that he hesitates before he answers.

"On your plans."

Blair huffs a nervous laugh.

"I don't want to overstay my welcome," they say cautiously.

Noah turns around. "You could never."

"Oh," Blair says eloquently, but Noah doesn't seem to mind their lack of communication skills. He simply serves the omelette and takes a seat opposite them, grinning from ear to ear. Blair shifts in their chair and takes a bite, humming in delight. "This is delish."

Noah smirks. "Happy you like it. There's more where this came from."

They dig in, both with a wide smile on their faces. 'Yes,' Blair thinks. 'A little commitment might not be as bad as I thought.'

WHAT'S IN A NAME

Jennifer puts the champagne bottle into the ice-filled cooler and checks the table arrangement for the last time. She shouldn't be so nervous, but she can't help it.

She runs her fingers over the black leather folder sitting in the centre of the table and then through her henna-dyed hair. The last time she saw Erin—just this morning—it had still been her natural dishwater blonde. But Erin is used to her impromptu decisions, loves her for it, even... may it be another tattoo or a spontaneous trip to Rome. Every time, Erin just smiles at her silly fiancée, kisses her, and lets her tell the story behind it.

Jennifer should be relaxed, but even after all these years, sometimes she still wonders if this one last thing might have been the straw that broke the camel's back. Yes, even when it is something as meaningless as changing the colour of her hair.

But she had just felt like it after this shitty morning. Maybe a thirty-something woman shouldn't dye her hair as an act of defiance, but her mother always loved her dirty blonde hair, loved that it was the same colour as her father's. Jennifer doesn't want to have any resemblance to him, though. It's enough that she has his eyes and his nose.

Jennifer pushes the thoughts away. It never does her any good when she thinks too long about family and stuff.

Thankfully, a key is shoved into the lock of the apartment door, and Jennifer smiles at the arrangement in front of her. The folder, candles, flower petals, a bottle of real champagne—maybe it's a bit over the top, but that's just how she is.

"Jenny?" Erin calls from the door. Jennifer's heart flutters a little. No one should still be so in love after four years in a relationship. Maybe it's the hormones. They often make her feel like a teenager.

"Dining room," she calls, and it only takes a second until Erin appears in the doorway. She stops, takes in her fiancée in her favourite summer dress, looking beautiful with her short now-ginger curls.

Jennifer's heart wants to beat out of her chest. "Hello, love," she says, nearly stumbling over the three syllables.

Erin walks closer and lays her hands on Jennifer's waist. "What's all that?" she asks, amusement clear in her voice.

Jennifer snickers, her cheeks dusting in a tender pink. She wraps her arms around Erin's neck and presses a soft kiss to her lips. She brushes her nose against Erin's and nods to a folder lying next to them on the festively set table.

Erin furrows her brow and opens it, the hand still resting on Jennifer's curling tighter when she sees the contents.

"Jen," she breathes and looks back at her, eyes wet with unspilt emotions.

Jennifer nods, her lips curling up into a smile as her eyes fill with tears. "In the flesh," she chuckles.

"You didn't need a piece of paper for that to be true," Erin points out.

"That might well be true, but..."

Erin nods in understanding. "Congratulations, darling," she says and pulls her fiancée into a tight embrace. "Well worth the champagne."

Jennifer beams at her. "I thought so."

Erin kisses her, puts in it how proud she is of her, how happy. She brushes a strand of hair out of Jennifer's face, smiles at her hair. "A new colour for the wedding?" she asks.

Jennifer chuckles. "I didn't think so far. Though every colour looks good with white, I guess."

"Every colour looks good on you, darling," Erin states, and it's so matter-of-factly that Jennifer has to believe it. Erin never tells white lies to butter anyone up. That's why Jennifer's mother hates her guts. That's why Jennifer loves her even more. Erin puts everyone, but especially her future mother-in-law, in their place whenever Jennifer is too tired to correct her as she calls her by a name that should have never been given to her in the first place.

"I made fettuccine con camarones," Jennifer chokes out around the ball of emotions in her throat.

Erin nods. It's such a simple movement, but her eyes and smile are full of understanding. She brushes her hands over Jennifer's sides. "Wonderful. I'm starving," she says and leans their foreheads together. "Does this count as a second birthday?"

Jennifer shakes her head. "No. That's when you first called me by my name. That was... special."

Erin nudges Jennifer's nose with her own. "It was my greatest pleasure, darling," she says and kisses her once more.

"Let's eat before the dinner turns cold and the champagne warm," Jennifer says, a little breathless when they part. She doesn't know what she did in a past life to deserve this, but the happiness that spreads through her chest is molten and warm, and it washes over the sharp edges of pain that linger everywhere. It may not last forever, but for this one moment, it will. And Jennifer will bathe in it as she enjoys her favourite meal with her favourite person and the bottle of champagne that she saved for this exact moment.

"To the future," Jennifer toasts her.

"To you, Jennifer," Erin replies and clinks their glasses together.

"To me," Jennifer agrees. "In the flesh, *and* on paper."

NIGHT LANDING

Ray looks up from his book, the light of his bedside lamp dipping his sharp features into soft orange colours.

"Hey, love," he says. "How was your evening?"

Yolanda leans her shoulder against the doorframe, her jeans jacket slung over the other as she smiles shyly. She's thankful that the darkness of the hallway is strong enough to cover up the blush crawling into her cheeks.

"Nice," she chuckles.

She's not sure if she'll ever get used to this. Coming home, smelling of sex and another person, their cologne or perfume sunken into her pores, the taste of their lips still lingering on hers—and Ray so utterly happy for her.

She knows he's been reading to distract himself, because that always works better for him than watching TV. She also knows that his worries and care are a sign of his love and an answer to what he used to believe to be a failure. But Yolanda knows better, and whenever doubts creep up on him, she wards them off with all the love she has for her spouse, infinite and unconditional.

For her, Ray is perfect—funny, intelligent, educated, and sexy. He always chuckles about the latter, though. That's okay. Not everyone agrees on what 'sexy' truly means. It stings now and then that he doesn't see her through this lens, but it only comes to the surface when she's insecure in other parts of her life. And if everything else fails – talking, cuddling, Ray giving her a massage – she goes out. Like today.

Getting ready is always a little weird. Ray truly doesn't

help by saying that *everything* looks great on her. Especially not when she looks at herself in the mirror with so much more scrutiny than she does when it comes to getting ready for a night out with her husband. Not that Ray doesn't care how she looks. He does. He simply thinks she's beautiful in everything, from threadbare home wear to evening dresses, with messy hair just as much as with a hairdo that took her half an hour to create. He compliments her on her looks, but she knows that the closest that comes to him finding her sexy is when she puts on the blue dress she wore when he asked her to marry him. She would never choose that one for a night like this. Never.

Ray closes his book and puts it on the nightstand before he stretches out his hand to beckon her near. A smile flickers over Yolanda's face, the gesture so familiar by now and still so big in the grand scheme of things.

She pushes off the doorframe and walks to his side of the bed, throwing her jacket on the chair that still holds the pile of dismissed outfits. She hears the clothes sliding down to the floor, but doesn't care. All that matters is reuniting with the man she loves after sharing her body with someone else.

She takes his hand. It's so warm in hers, so familiar. It never stops to amaze her how a single, simple touch can connect them, how Ray's smile is what she longs for all the way home, his arms, his strong chest, his breath on her skin.

She longs for many things. But for one thing, she hasn't longed for in a very long time: for him to be different.

She sits down on the mattress and presses a soft kiss on Ray's lips. Their noses bump together, and a shared chuckle makes it even worse. Yolanda leans her forehead against Ray's, her snicker sending short puffs of air against his skin. They kiss again, slow and with relish, his hands in her hair, her fingers trailing over his sides.

"I love you," Yolanda whispers into his lips. Ray smiles too wide after that to keep on kissing.

"I love you, too," he returns and adds, "I missed you." It's honest, and it could be heartbreaking. But strangely, it isn't.

"Same. Time that I get ready for bed and catch up on what I missed out on while I was gone."

She rises from the bed and walks to the bathroom, brushes her teeth and takes her evening shower. Naked as the day she was born, she strolls back into the bedroom. Ray glances up from the pages of his book when she enters, but just for a second. Yolanda chuckles quietly to herself and shakes her head. She remembers the other man's eyes wandering over her skin tonight with adoration and lust. It felt good, being perceived like that. A thrill that boosted her mood and self-perception and left her satisfied and sated after looks morphed into hands and lips.

It's something that Ray can't give her, just like she can't share his love for brass music, no matter how talented her husband might be on the trombone. He doesn't love her any less for not enjoying his hobby.

Yolanda never thought that she would ever find someone, who would love her with all her quirks, who could want to bridge differences without asking for sacrifices. Ray didn't, either. Maybe that's why they take on every challenge as a team, don't see bumps in the road as insurmountable problems. It's what makes them so good together. It's what makes them the couple many around them strive to be.

Ray looks up from his book when Yolanda slips under

the covers in his favourite pyjamas. He once told her that the colour suited her and that he loved the fabric because it was just as cuddly as herself. She always wears it on nights like this. And he always smiles at her in a way that she knows that he knows.

Ray stretches his arm out, and Yolanda follows the silent invitation.

"Tired?" he asks.

Yolanda hums her reply where her face is pressed against his shoulder and inhales his scent. She cuddles closer until they touch as much as possible, a sigh of contentment falling from her lips.

"Good night," Ray whispers and presses a kiss into her hair.

"Night," she mumbles before she slides into sleep. She doesn't hear Ray's soft chuckle anymore or feel his tender gaze on her. He hugs her a little closer nonetheless and returns to his book.

A CROCK OF GOLD

Eric lets the keys fall into the key bowl that his tidy boyfriend put on the sideboard in their entrance hall. His bag slips off his shoulder, crashing down with a loud *thump*. David will scold him for getting just another dent in his thermos bottle, but Eric is too tired to even care. His last client was a nightmare, taking double the time allocated, and if he's absolutely honest, he just wants to curl up in his bed and sleep for two days straight.

It's been a long week, and sending David the don't-wait-for-me text hurt more than he is willing to admit. Work is eating him up and spitting him out, and his boyfriend gets the unsavoury remains.

Eric knows he lets out his frustration on David. Last night they fought so loud that Mrs Wahyu hit the ceiling with a broomstick.

Eric doesn't want to fight, but he can just imagine what is waiting for him beyond the hallway. Anger, maybe? Or the silent treatment? Friday nights are holy. *Were* holy. Now he's crashed date night thrice in a row. Whatever David will unleash on him, he deserves it.

Fear curls razor-sharp through his stomach. He doesn't want to hurt his boyfriend, doesn't want their relationship to head south. But he doesn't know how to make this work. The business is hanging on a thread. If he wants to keep it operating in the black, he needs to work long hours. There's no financial wriggle room to hire more people.

Eric slips out of his shoes and walks into their dimly lit kitchen-diner. The table is set beautifully, the candles not lit yet, but a bottle of his favourite red wine is already breathing in a decanter. David taught him to like more than beer and whiskey.

It smells like food is still on the stove, but it's empty as far as he can see. Eric worries his lip between his teeth. Did David leave in frustration?

"Dave?" he more croaks than calls. No answer. "David?" he tries louder.

"Coming. Just give me a sec."

Eric breathes out in relief. David sounds good-tempered even though he really shouldn't. It's past nine. Eric should have been here at six.

"Hello, Eric." The familiar greeting washes away some of the dread tightening his chest. David cups the back of his head and kisses him. Eric flinches in surprise, sobs quietly into his partner's lips. "Shh. Don't. We're good."

Eric pulls back and looks at him warily.

"Are we?"

David breathes a sigh.

"Yes. We are. I know you don't do this to get away from me."

He gives him a close-lipped smile.

Eric shakes his head.

"I hate Mitchell. I wish we could afford to lose him as a client."

"I know."

Eric furrows his brow.

"Why are you so...?"

"Understanding?"

Eric nods.

"I don't want us to spend the little time we have fighting. I'm frustrated, but none of us feels better just because we talk it to death. This project will end, eventually. But I don't want us to just survive until then."

Eric breathes a sigh of relief and kisses him softly. They lean their foreheads together.

"I love you," Eric whispers.

David pecks his lips and smiles.

"I love you, too. Come on. I'm starving. And surely you are, too."

Eric nods and pulls his boyfriend into a tight hug. He presses a kiss into David's hair before he lets go of him.

"What's for dinner?"

David turns and walks to the far side of the kitchen where he switches on the light underneath the cabinet.

Eric chuckles.

"You found my mother's crockpot?"

David chuckles.

"No more drying or cooling food when you come home late. I learnt my lesson."

There is not a hint of heat lacing the words, and Eric relaxes further. He stares at David's back for a long moment, then pulls the matches out of a drawer and lights the candles. David puts the slow cooker's ceramic bowl in the middle of the table and serves each of them a generous helping of lasagna.

"You're an angel," Eric says and moans around the first forkful. "This is *so* good."

David smiles and pours wine into their glasses.

"I hope you don't miss the crunchy cheese on top."

Eric grins over the rim of his wine glass.

"This is perfect."

The 'you are perfect' hangs unspoken between them, but Eric knows David can hear it. He was always good in looking through all the layers Eric shows to the world to his very core, the unmasked Eric—sensitive, vulnerable, loving without boundaries.

They eat mostly in silence, fingers woven together as they enjoy the dessert.

"This was nice," David states when they finished it off.

Eric nods.

"My mum used to cook stew in the crock pot when I was a little kid. I must check her cookbook. She used to write down all her recipes, you know?"

David smiles. Eric can hear the unspoken 'Just a million times'.

"Maybe I could prepare dinner in the morning so that you don't always have to cook," Eric muses.

David shakes his head.

"It's not a chore, love."

"I know. But you deserve a free evening now and then, don't you think?"

David gets up, carries the plates to the sink and opens the tap.

"I wouldn't mind."

Eric brings the pot to him and pulls David into his arms, kissing him while the water fills the sink. They only take a quick break to turn the tap off and stop when David needs to yawn.

"Go get ready for bed, love," Eric says. "I'll handle the dishes."

David nods and presses a peck to his boyfriend's cheek.

"Join me when you're done," he says.
Eric brushes their noses together.
"I'll be with you in a minute."

BUTTERFLIES

Sophie gets off the bus right in front of St Michael's. A warm summer breeze blows her long, flowy dress against her legs, and the warmth of the afternoon sun sinks into the skin of her bare arms.

St. Michael's is the congregation her best friend Emmy has been a member of since childhood. Sophie has never really gone to services since her husband died. She couldn't forgive a god who took her beloved Frank away, aged 57.

But now she's here, six years later, under the pressure of Emmy, who invited her to join her and her 'gang' in the senior dance. As if she were an old woman. She had scoffed at the suggestion, but here she is, 61, in a long flowy, sleeveless dress that seems to scream, 'I'm not one of you.' But as she quickly learns, she most definitely is. Of course, there are the 80+ couples in their Sunday best, but also people her age, dressed just as young as herself. Maybe it's not so bad after all.

The music is a nice mix of old and new. The DJ keeps it in the discofox and slow dance department, and it's not too loud to drown out the conversations happening at the borders of the makeshift dance floor and along the buffet that seems to be the main attraction for some of the folks attending.

Emmy waves at her from the canapé section of the buffet table, and Sophie sighs, not sure if in relief or defeat. She knows her friend means well, but Emmy can't take no for an answer. It's enough to drive her up the wall sometimes, but their friendship spans nearly five decades now. She will never find someone as kind and infuriating as her, who knows how to handle her when times are rough and makes her laugh so hard that her lungs are burning when life is good.

She greets her friend with a hug and waves to Emmy's acquaintances before loading her plate with goodies. Yes, maybe she came because of the praised food. Sue her.

Sophie takes a seat at the table where Emmy and her boyfriend, Albert, are already sitting. He's a good man, treats her friend right. But he's also the source of Emmy's undying drive to play matchmaker for Sophie. As if life would only be fulfilling if you have a partner.

It's not as if Sophie wouldn't agree to the premise if Frank were still alive. But he sadly isn't.

She lets her gaze wander over the dancing couples, filling her mouth with cheese and grapes as she only half-listens to Emmy's latest gossip.

It doesn't take long until the first man asks her for a dance. She accepts, if only to get away from the uhs and ahs welling up around her.

The man, Karim, is a good dancer and smells like tobacco and lemon. She steps on his feet a few times, which he always answers with an amused chuckle and after the song, he leads her back to the table and asks another woman to dance.

Sophie chuckles. That wasn't *too* bad. Emmy voices her thoughts as if plucking them directly from her head, and Sophie has to agree that she's having fun.

A few other men ask her on the dance floor, some more talented than others, some more respectful than others, but after an hour of dancing, Sophie's stomach aches from laughing and her feet hurt in the most delicious way.

She puts them up on an empty chair and watches, leaning

her head against the wall behind her. She finds herself smiling, her heart light as a feather. For a moment, she closes her eyes and listens to the pop song coming over the loudspeakers, the low hum of people talking over the music, the few people singing along. It's nice, peaceful.

"Excuse me?" someone asks quietly, and even before Sophie opens her eyes, she pulls her feet off the chair, a steadying hand on the table. She chuckles to herself. Well, one doesn't get younger.

"Hi, I'm Martine. May I have the next dance?" the gentle voice asks, and Sophie looks up. The woman looking down at her with the brightest smile she has ever seen waits patiently as Sophie collects herself.

"Um."

Emmy shoves her shoulder unceremoniously.

"Many women dance together here. We always have a surplus," she says, and Sophie wishes she had put proper make-up on today. Maybe that would have managed to cover up the heat shooting into her cheeks.

"That's not the only reason why a woman might ask another woman for a dance," Martine says calmly, her eyes sparkling and never leaving Sophie's face.

Sophie moves her lips, words failing her. God, even as a teen she had been so bad at flirting with girls. She fancied them and some fancied her back, but she was a babbling disaster every time a girl so much as looked at her. Four decades later and she hasn't changed one bit. Just perfect.

Martine still smiles at her, waiting her out while the whole table falls silent. Sophie feels eyes on her, but the only pair that counts is Martine's brown gaze, lingering on her, warm like a caress. And Sophie feels her hand moving of its own accord to accept Martine's, realising way too late that the other woman didn't offer hers in the first place.

But Martine remedies that quickly, takes Sophie's hand in her own and presses a kiss on its back. Sophie blushes impossibly deeper and snickers like the teenage girl she's regressed to be.

Martine leads her to the dance floor, still smiling softly. Sophie is grateful when Martine's right hand lands on her hip. She's worried enough about the woman's toes. Trying to figure out how to lead would surely end in disaster.

"Relax," Martine whispers. "I'm not gonna bite you."

Sophie chuckles and leans into the touch, a smile playing on her face. It hurts a little as wide as it is, but she welcomes it. Martine beams back at her.

"I couldn't take my eyes off of you," she confesses. "You look lovely."

"Thank you," Sophie snickers.

"Have you ever danced with a woman?" Martine asks and pulls her closer.

"Not since I was sixteen," she replies, voice breathy as her heart beats faster and faster.

Martine smells delicious, like lilac and a summer breeze. Her dark hair frames her neck beautifully, and Sophie needs to remind herself to breathe as Martine leads her over the dancefloor with ease, not showing the slightest hint of Sophie stepping on her toes.

The music fades, and Sophie pulls back like so many times today. But Martine's hand is still resting in hers, and Sophie doesn't want to let go, doesn't want this to end.

The new, slow song begins, and they are still standing there, looking into each other's eyes, an unknown spell shielding them from the ado around them.

"May I have the next dance?" Sophie asks through the heart in her mouth, and Martine's face breaks into a bright smile, putting the sun to shame.

"With pleasure," she says, and Sophie wraps her arms boldly around Martine's neck.

Later, when Sophie sits down on the seat of the bus, her feet numb and her heart full, the sun already dipping down behind the city, she opens the new contact on her phone and looks at Martine's smile.

Butterflies. Who would have thought that they feel just the same at sixteen and sixty-one?

IN THE EYE OF THE BEHOLDER

Sally never liked her body. She grew up hearing all the time that she was too podgy, that she should do more with her hair, that she should wear other glasses, stuff like that. She was taught to eat all the food on her plate even after being full, just to hear comments on her widening hips and growing breasts later. They weren't positive. The overeating it ingrained in her isn't either.

Sally is 35 now, and if someone would ask, she would describe her body as a scene of battle. It has scars and stretch marks, a fat apron, and is well-padded throughout. Her face is a deep red at all times. Couperose is a bitch. Her arms are slim, though. Maybe that's why she likes them the most.

She lost a lot of weight, hopefully for good this time. Her face looks slimmer, but she only sees it when she's really looking. She tries to avoid that unless she is tying her headwraps. The mirror isn't her enemy, but it isn't her friend either.

Today is a good day, though, and she likes the woman who smiles back at her in the reflection. She's wearing the best good-looking shapewear she could afford, her favourite little black dress that covers her knees and elbows and falls just right to accentuate her hourglass figure. It makes her new red shoes and the pomegranate necklace she's wearing stand out.

Sally is glad that for a change, she's feeling good in her own skin because today, she has a date with Nora and after the more than hot makeout session last time, Sally is pretty sure this time they will go all the way.

Sally is nervous. Not because of Nora. No. She's the sweetest woman she has ever met. She's her age, and she is breathtakingly beautiful. Her eyes shine like emeralds, her nose is so pretty, peppered with freckles just like her cheeks, and so gentle rubbing against Sally's when they are kissing.

Her lips. Sally could write poems about her lips—how soft they are, how gentle they kiss, how they taste like summer and everything good. They form the most beautiful smiles, too.

Nora is Sally's first girlfriend and her first partner after she divorced her husband Andy after nearly two decades together. High-school sweethearts they had been, but their burning love had simmered down after three kids and finally died out. It wasn't anybody's fault. They both let it happen. They parted as friends.

Afterwards, Sally went out on many dates with men, women and non-binary folks. She was surprised that they were even marginally interested in her. But mid-thirties seemed to often start anew, so Sally jumped right into the dating world, got her heart semi-broken several times—until she met Nora.

Nora with the red curls and green eyes, with her hearty laugh and cheeky comments that make Sally giddy with love and giggling like a teenager.

Nora, who doesn't mind that she has never been with a woman before, who tells Sally how beautiful and special she is, how talented and smart. Nora, who looks at her as if she really means all these words.

Sally still thinks it's too good to be true, but she decided that even the worst heartbreak would be worth a minute in Nora's arms.

Sally tugs on her dress and smoothens it out, runs her hand over the soft fabric of her turban, puts in her pomegranate earrings and mascara on her lashes.

She confessed how much she hated make-up on their very first date, and Nora insisted on her coming without it to their second date. Sally complied and got the most beautiful smile in response. Her cheeks may have burnt even more crimson than usual, but Nora kissed them gently.

Nora promised to cook for her tonight, and now, Sally knocks at her door. But dinner is forgotten as soon as it opens, and Sally soaks her in. She is a sight to behold. Nora's jeans hang low and her shirt rides up when she cups Sally's face to kiss her gently, giving free view to a small stripe of smooth skin.

It should raise the anticipation for dessert, but all Sally feels is dread. What was she thinking? She knows that Nora kept a steady weight through the years and had no kids. She shouldn't be surprised that she can get away with tight clothes without pressing herself into Spanx, but somehow the fact is still catching her on the hop.

The delicious dinner and Nora's entertaining skills take her mind off the worry, but as soon as Nora leads her to her couch, it's back in full swing.

"Are you alright? You seem tense," Nora asks softly and Sally can't meet her eyes. She should just leave now. But she can't. Nora is right here, and her lips are so damn inviting.

Sally shakes her head and cards a hand absentmindedly through Nora's hair. "I'm fine. Just ...," she breathes out sharply, "nervous."

"Why?" Nora asks ever so gently.

Sally gives her a timid smile. "Because you're perfect and

I'm... so very not."

Nora knits her brow together. "What makes you think that?"

Sally can't find words to describe her inner turmoil, for how shame crawls over her skin and makes it feel two sizes too small. How could she voice her fear of rejection or even worse—humiliation?

So she runs her fingertips tenderly over Nora's skin above her waistband. Vulnerable blue eyes find green understanding ones. Nora brushes her thumb over Sally's cheek. "It's me," she simply says, and there is assurance and love wrapped up in this small sentence.

"I know," Sally whispers, barely audible, "but I am me."

Nora hums in response and waits. As much as she can talk one's ears off, she knows when to wait until someone is ready to talk.

Sally needs some time to say, "I want you."

Nora smiles at her. "I want you, too."

Sally shakes her head. "You have *no* idea what you are getting yourself into," she chuckles self-depreciatingly.

"Neither do you," Nora replies, her voice still soft, but with an edge of pain. Sally doesn't know what to make of it.

Nora takes her hand and pulls her off the sofa. "This isn't a conversation for the living room. Come."

She leads her to her bedroom and switches on the bedside lamp that throws a soft light, leaving most of the room in dark shadows. She pulls Sally down to sit next to her on the edge of her bed.

Nora grabs Sally's chin tenderly and pushes it softly to meet her eyes. "You are beautiful," Nora says. Her girlfriend huffs in lieu of an answer. "You. Are. Beautiful," Nora repeats. "Didn't Andy ever tell you how beautiful you are?"

It's a low blow, Nora knows that, but how else is she meant to take Sally's fear away?

"He did find me... beautiful. Even after I had the kids."

"Of course he did," Nora says, a smile lacing her voice.

"He's known me since I was sixteen. I'm sure he didn't love my body how it is now. It's just attachment and history..."

Nora shushes her. "No. I'm sure he saw you at that moment, and he found you beautiful the way you were."

Sally lets the words sink in. No, that can't be true.

Nora's hands wander over her dress and stop at the hem. "May I?" she asks, waiting for Sally's consent. She takes a deep breath and nods.

Sally stands up, and Nora pushes the dress way up to her neck. Both start laughing when it gets stuck on Sally's headwrap.

"Maybe I should take this off first," Sally snickers. Nora looks at her in awe. She has never seen her girlfriend unwrapped before. She knows it's something Sally would only do in front of her family or her spouse. This is a big step, maybe even a bigger gift than nakedness could be.

She watches Sally push the wrap backwards and off, sees her dark blond, messy bun and the light curls that fall into her face. Sally lets her hair down, literally.

She pulls her dress over her head and runs her hand through her long hair. All Nora can think is how incredibly beautiful she is. She tells her so.

Sally blushes and looks down at herself. Shapewear is rarely pretty and the lace band bites into her thighs. But there is

Nora's hand on her chin again, and soft lips pepper little kisses all over her face until they find her mouth.

Nora is such a good kisser, and soon, Sally feels dizzy, intoxicated by her gorgeous girlfriend and a slight lack of oxygen.

Nora takes her hands and puts them on her own hips, waiting for Sally to find the courage to undress her, too.

Sally moves her thumbs slowly under the shirt and explores the skin beneath the fabric. Then she pushes it up and over Nora's head.

Her hand runs over the freckle dusted chest. She wants to map them out, find constellations in them, connecting the dots. But her hand stills and she looks up at her girlfriend, green eyes meeting blue.

"I always was insecure about my freckles and my ginger hair. Kids bullied me in school, and even as an adult, I heard the word 'witch' more than once," Nora states as if it weren't the strangest thing Sally has ever heard from her mouth.

"I think they are exceptionally beautiful," Sally whispers.

"Thank you. I bet I find a lot of beauty underneath this, too," Nora says, running her hand over the sleek synthetic of Sally's underwear.

Sally's breath quivers. Her heart is nearly beating out of her chest, and her hands get cold. It's now or never. She pulls the underdress upwards, getting herself caught in the tightness, trying to get it over her shoulders.

She hears Nora chuckling and wishes the ground would open up and swallow her whole. Then she feels movement and hands that help her out of her misery. Nora kisses her in an instant, grounding her with her lips and the hands on her hips.

Sally kisses back. If it's the last time she feels these lips on hers, she'd better savour it.

She feels Nora's hands gliding over her body, one finding its way into her hair the other under her lace panties. "Nora," she gasps into her mouth and the hands stop still.

"Too fast?" her girlfriend asks, but Sally shakes her head. "Then what is it?"

Sally looks down and idly plays with the waistband of Nora's jeans. "Could you take a look at my body? I couldn't survive it if you..." she trails off.

Nora cups her face and kisses her, long and slow. She takes a step back then, scanning Sally from top to bottom, slowly, diligently. She runs her fingers over the lines on Sally's hip and the hem of her panties, over the fat apron that oozes out of them.

"Your body tells the story of your life, and I can't wait for you to tell me every joy and every pain that created these lines and scars. But," she runs her fingers over the small of Sally's back and pulls her closer, "first, I need to feel you, head to toe. What do you say?"

Sally smiles gingerly and pops the button of Nora's jeans open. "I'd say that you're not only beautiful, but really, really smart."

Nora smirks at her. "I must be. You wouldn't date a boob."

Sally laughs out loud. "You didn't just say that!?"

Nora shrugs her shoulders in fake innocence, turns around, and pushes her jeans down. She climbs under the covers and holds them up in a silent invitation. Sally can't help but beam at her. The saying is right. Beauty *is* in the eye of the beholder.

TRUTH

'Oh, shit. It's going to be tight tomorrow,' Tim thinks as he licks up Peter's cock and takes the tip into his mouth. 'Why does Charlotte need this stupid birthday cake from the other side of town?'

He knows why. Even a pie lover like Tim has to admit that *Angel's Sweets* makes the best fancy cakes in the area. But his schedule is already full to the brim, and Charlotte breaking her foot right before her big birthday party comes at an unfortunate time.

Tim takes Peter deep into his mouth. God, he loves the sounds his boyfriend makes, the hand in his hair—never guiding, just another point of contact—the way his body strains in an attempt not to fuck his throat sore.

Peter is always so careful with him. Tim loves to unleash the dragon, though, to make his boyfriend lose his constraints. Peter once told him that he never had the chance to show this part of himself in past relationships. Maybe Tim is a bit smug about it. Sue him.

Tim ponders his options to take a bit off the next day's stress. Maybe, when Peter has fallen asleep in post-orgasmic bliss, he could get up and prepare the pasta salad and the burger patties. Better late at night than early in the morning.

He circles Peter's hole with a finger, probing a little. Peter always comes so much quicker with a bit of anal play. Usually,

Tim loves to draw it all out, but he had a damn long week, and he's tired. Quickies are okay if they don't become the norm, right?

Tim still hasn't figured out what 'normal' means regarding sex. Statistics will always only get you so far. So he decided to let his boyfriend of nine months take the lead, and at the moment, they have sex three to four times a week.

His finger slips in easily, and he moves it carefully inside his boyfriend. Peter for sure is a goner today, his legs already twitching. Tim loves it. Loves to make Peter feel good.

"If you keep on doing this, I'll come," Peter pants above him, and Tim smirks around his cock.

He pulls off and grins. "Don't you wanna?"

Peter chuckles. "Sure. But would you fuck me tonight?"

Okay, no quickie then. "Sure, babe." Tim presses a kiss into the soft flesh of Peter's thigh and pushes himself up to kiss him on the lips. He loses himself in it before his hand sneaks down to his semi-hard dick and pulls a few times until it's filling out. He fetches the lube from the bedside drawer and starts opening Peter up. His fingers glide with ease, and as always, Tim is in awe with how quickly his boyfriend can be prepped. He himself always needs more coaxing.

It's not that he doesn't like it. Peter is always so good to him. It's probably just the pressure to come that makes him tense. But there are so many beautiful things that hands, mouths, and gliding bodies can create that the times they've done it anal still wouldn't count up on all his fingers.

Peter is putty under his ministrations, and it doesn't take long after Tim pushes inside him for Peter to come with Tim's hand on his cock and his name on his beautiful lips.

Tim pulls out before Peter emerges on the other side, his erection already flagging. He tries to get up to get a wet washcloth but Peter paws at him. "Cuddles," he whines, and Tim chuckles as he falls back into bed and wraps himself around his sex-drunk lover.

He loves cuddling, but after sex, he always feels a little overwhelmed by it. Probably a state of being overtouched. But Peter's wish is his command, and it doesn't take long before he's snoring quietly above him anyway. Tim cleans him up before he covers him with a blanket and goes to work in the kitchen. A well-infused pasta salad is better than a fresh one anyway.

Morning comes way too early. Tim grumbles something unintelligible as he tries to swipe away the alarm for the third time. The bed is empty next to him. How one can be an early bird, Tim will never understand. But he sure as hell won't complain if it means that the man of his dreams brings him fresh coffee in bed.

"Good morning, love," Peter says and presses a kiss to his temple. "Drink up. Long day ahead."

Tim groans. "Don't remind me."

Peter chuckles. "I see you've already prepared our savoury food."

Tim hums. "You gonna bake today?"

Peter nods. "Yes. My double chocolate muffins and something new—lemon muffins with poppy seeds."

"You're lucky that I love you even with black bits between your teeth." Tim chuckles.

"I'm lucky that you love me. Period."

Even before his morning coffee, Tim softens under the words. "Me, too."

Tim hates the city centre on Saturdays. Everyone seems to be out and about, and he's already twenty minutes late for the cake pickup. But he's stuck in traffic. *Great.*

His phone ringing doesn't raise his mood until he sees it's Charlotte. "Hey, what's up, sis?" he asks over speakerphone.

"Um, fine. Everything's fine."

Tim knows his little sister way too well to believe this lie. "What happened?"

"Well, nothing bad, I hope. Um... you know that I invited everyone via email?"

"Yes, you even sent one to me."

Charlotte chuckles, but it sounds strained. "Yeah. Um... I simply used the same group-header as last year. It's always the same people anyway. But I forgot..."

Tim hits the breaks and shouts at the man who stepped in front of his car without looking. "Sorry, Charlotte. You said what?"

"I forgot to take Anne off the mailing list."

Tim stares at the red light in front of him. He hasn't seen Anne since they broke up ten months ago. *Shit!*

"I only realised when she texted me birthday wishes at midnight and asked what she should bring today."

Tim exhales audibly. "And what did you say?"

There is a long pause before Charlotte answers. "I panicked and said pasta salad."

Tim groans. "I said that I'd bring it. And it's Anne's recipe, so she'll probably bring the same."

"I'm sorry, Tim. I can disinvite her."

Tim white-knuckles the steering wheel. "Nah. We're adults. I guess she's ready to be around me again. Which is good."

"Have you seen each other since the break-up?"

Tim shakes his head. "No. She said she needed space. It's gonna be fine, Charlotte. I gotta go now. Your birthday cake is waiting."

Tim flips another burger and tries hard not to look at Anne, who just arrived with a big hello welcoming her. He never bad-mouthed her so nobody harbours a grudge. They all know he's happy with Peter anyway.

Anne makes her rounds, and Tim is still busy grilling burgers when she finally approaches him.

"Hey, Tim."

He smiles at her. It comes easily despite the contradicting emotions battling in his stomach. "Hey, Anny. Hungry?"

She nods and hands him her plate. "You're looking good," she states.

Heat shoots into Tim's cheeks. Surely just the barbecue grill. "Thanks. You—" She looks so thin. He knows her well enough to know that isn't a good sign. "I heard your art studio is doing great."

She smiles at him. Tim's hand twitches with the urge to brush a loose strand of hair behind her ear. Muscle memory is a strange thing.

"Yeah. I'm doing alright. It's enough to get by."

"I'm happy for you, Anny. I know it was always your dream."

She presses her lips together and nods. They stay silent for an awkwardly long moment. Everyone seems to be keeping their distance for their reunion. Even Peter is talking with Stevie on the other side of the lawn. Trish is looking ostentatiously in the other direction. Tim knows she would never read their lips, but he appreciates the gesture.

Anne pushes her hands into the pockets of her jeans and worries her lip. "I thought a lot about you over the last few months. About *us*." Tim looks up from the burgers. "I had hoped that Charlotte inviting me to her birthday meant you would probably..."

Tim's blood runs cold. Doesn't Anne know that he and Peter are together? She must have heard it through the grapevine. Tim sure knows about the men she dated since they went their different ways.

"I miss you, Tim. I know, I messed up. This... I took something beautiful and destroyed it."

"Anny."

"No, please. Let me finish. I'm sorry that I hurt you. I read a lot about it. I'm much more informed now, and I understand that I did you wrong in assuming that you weren't really in love with me. I always thought that sex was the basis of true love, and I thought being ace meant hating it. I didn't believe you, and for that, I'm sorry."

Tim nods. "It's alright, Anny. I blew it. Should've kept it to myself."

She puts a hand on his arm. "I don't want you to hide. I went with you to pride, didn't I? I'm not ashamed of you. I didn't understand then that it was no different to being straight or pan. But I do now. If you can forgive me, maybe we could start over again?"

Tim stares at her hand for a long moment. "I'm with Pete

now," he says and glances up.

Surprise washes over Anne's face, and she takes a step back. "Oh."

Tim nods. "Yeah."

"Are... are you happy?"

Tim smiles. "Yes, we are."

She chuckles. It sounds forced. "Well, you two danced around each other for years."

"Yes. First time that both of us were single." He puts a burger on her bun and hands her plate over.

Anne looks over to Peter, their eyes meeting. "I'm happy that he is more understanding than I was." Her eyes grow glassy with unshed tears. "You deserve someone who accepts you, who embraces and loves you just as you are."

Tim nods, biting the inside of his lip. "Yeah. I mean, I learnt from the mistakes I made in our relationship."

Anne furrows her brow. "You did nothing wrong, Tim."

Tim chuckles self-deprecatingly. "We had a good thing going, Anny, and then I dropped the ace bomb, destroying everything. I won't repeat that."

Anne's eyes grow wide. "He doesn't know? He's been your best friend for over a decade! How did you explain to him why we broke up?"

"I told him the truth. That we weren't meant to be. He's not one to poke."

Anne shakes her head. "But he deserves to know. You can't just hide that from your boyfriend."

"Hide what?" Peter asks. None of them saw him coming.

Shit! Shit! Shit!

"Nothing, babe."

Peter's eyes flicker between the two exes. He sets his jaw and takes a breath. "We'll talk later then. Nice to see you again, Anne." Peter turns and walks inside the house. Tim's shoulders slump.

"I'm so sorry, Tim," Anne says.

"Thanks a lot, Anny. Way to destroy my happiness," Tim grunts.

"I didn't mean to..."

"Yeah. You never do." He unties his apron and throws it on the table next to the grill. "Stevie, will ya take over the barbecue?"

"Sure, boss."

Tim pats him on his back and hurries into the house. He finds Peter in the kitchen, talking with Trish. Their hands are signing too quickly for Tim to understand, but both are laughing. *Good.*

He presses a kiss on Peter's cheek. His heart clenches when his boyfriend gives him an unreadable look instead of a smile as he usually does. This is going to be a long day.

Tim wakes up with the hangover of the century. He's gonna die for sure. But his angel left painkillers and water on his bedside table. And a note. Tim needs a moment to make his brain work to be able to read it.

Out for a run. P

Tim stares at the small paper. No doodles, no 'I love you'. And then, there's the fact that Peter never goes out running on a Sunday morning. This is their lazy day. They sleep in, have sex, share a shower, and then walk to the small café around the corner offering scones and pie all day. Not that he would crave any of it right now.

He takes the pills and swallows them. He can't even remember how they got home. He hasn't been wasted like that in years. Why did he shoot himself off like that?

He slumps into his pillow and turns slowly on his side. Maybe Peter will fill in the blanks later.

The next time he wakes up, there is another dose of painkillers on his nightstand and quiet noises of clattering tableware coming from the kitchen. Peter's back. Tim smiles despite the headache still drumming in his head. He swallows the pills and slowly shuffles to the kitchen. "Morning," he croaks.

"Good afternoon," Peter replies, but there is no teasing tone accompanying it.

"Sorry you had to drag me up the stairs. I'm sure I was a dead weight."

"Yes. A very talkative one, though." Peter throws a tea bag into his mug. Peter never drinks that stuff. He's the connoisseur of loose teas.

"Are you alright, babe?"

Peter huffs a humourless laugh. "You tell me, Timothy 'I'm not attracted to my boyfriend' Cox. You tell me."

Tim feels nausea washing through his stomach like a tidal wave. What the hell did he tell him last night?

"Wha... what do you mean?"

Peter leans against the kitchen cabinets and regards him for a long, painful moment. "You said you didn't want to fuck anyone. That was... a surprise, as I had the impression you rather enjoyed sleeping with me. But I was delusional, I suppose."

"Pete, I can explain."

"Oh, you already did. In way too much graphic detail. I really didn't need you to spell out the sexual activities you had with your exes. I'm not a prude, but woah!" Peter's annoyance oozes out of every fibre of his being.

"I'm so sorry."

"About what? That you lied to me? That my best friend and lover only feigned liking having sex with me? Or is there something else we can add to the list?" Tim clicks his mouth shut and wills the tears welling up in his eyes to retract. Peter shakes his head. "I'll be in my study." He takes his mug and brushes past Tim.

Fuck!

Tim tries to see it as a positive sign that Peter didn't chuck him out on his ear. He decides to give him space.

He grabs his phone. Several missed calls and a ton of text messages await him. His eyes grow wider and wider as he scrolls through them.

Are you okay?

I'm so sorry. Tell me if I can help you in any way.

It's okay, dude. You're perfect and deserving of love like anyone else.

Hope you're fine.

What the hell happened!? Why can't he remember a single thing? Before he can think better of it, he dials Charlotte's number. His sister picks up after a second.

"Hey, brother dear. How're you doing?"

"Hangover. 'm fine."

"Really?"

Tim swallows hard and runs a hand over his face. "What happened last night?"

Charlotte laughs. It hurts Tim's head. "Better ask what didn't happen last night."

"How bad was it?"

Charlotte exhales sharply. "You came out to the whole party as ace and took great effort to let everyone know that you take good care of all of your lovers. Sexually."

"Fuck!"

"Yeah, that's what it was mostly about." Charlotte laughs.

Tim groans and slumps on the sofa. "I'm so sorry, Charlotte. I didn't mean to crash your birthday."

There's a long pause on the other side, and Tim prays that Charlotte is simply signing to Trish, and not that he broke something irreparably between them. She's the only family he's got left, and if Peter breaks up with him... He can't even think clearly after that thought.

"I'm proud of you that you came out to us. It must have been hard to keep this part of you bottled up. I'm sorry that it happened in a way you couldn't really control. We tried to shut you up, but..."

Tim nods, regretting it immediately. *Stupid hangover!*

"How... how did Peter react when I said it?"

"You haven't talked with him yet?"

Tim winces, but this time, not from pain. "Not really. He's in his study."

"You mean *your* study."

Tim deflates. "He called it his, so chances are high we have to carry my old desk down again soon. Or I leave it with him. It's never been my style."

"Tim. He won't break up with you. He loves you way too much."

"Didn't hold back Anne," Tim points out.

"But he's not Anne. He was shocked, like all of us. But I'm sure you two can talk it out."

"I hope you're right, Charlotte. Thanks."

Tim finds Peter at his desk, the laptop screen mirroring in his glasses. "Can we talk?"

Peter looks up from the computer. "Have you ever loved me or was I just a weird rebound?"

Tim gapes at him. "Pete, you could never... Of course, I love you. My sexuality has nothing to do with my feelings for you."

Peter nods and leans back in his chair. "Then why didn't you just tell me?"

Tim slumps against the doorframe and pushes his thumbs into the waistband of his pyjama pants. "Because it would hurt you like it did Anne, and I didn't want to lose you."

It sounds lame and egoistic, but it's the truth. Peter seems to see that. "But you had sex with me, all this time. I feel like I violated you without even knowing."

"You didn't. Listen... I don't have a problem with having sex. Never had. That's why it took me nearly forty years to come out to myself. And the first one I told was Anne, and you know how that ended."

Peter pushes his jaw forward and nods. "Still... I thought you trusted me with everything. I was your friend then, wasn't I?" His eyes look tired and red when he fixes them on Tim's gaze.

"It's not like coming out as gay or pan. Most people get that you can't help but fall in love with someone of your own gender if you're wired like that. But outing myself as ace always brings questions about my partner. I didn't want to bring Anny or you into a situation to be questioned about what we do or not do, or for others to pity you."

"I don't care what others think. That's none of their goddamn business!" Peter all but shouts. Tim winces. Peter barely curses. "Didn't you know that I would love this part of you just like I love every other? All the wonderful and infuriating parts that make one beautiful Tim Cox?"

Tim needs to look away. He feels like shattering into a million pieces. "Will you break up with me?" he asks, his voice as thin as cheap parchment paper.

There is no answer, and Tim closes his eyes. This is it. If he can't even keep Peter – the man who has been in love with him for a decade and still didn't leave his side – then lasting love will never find him.

He hears the desk chair scratching over the wooden floor and carpet-muffled steps walking towards the door. He wants to beg and plead. But he deserves this. Peter is right. He lied to him. He didn't trust him enough. *Him!* And now, he has lost his love.

But Peter doesn't push him out of the way. Instead, gentle thumbs run over Tim's stubble, and tender lips brush over his own. Tim is frozen to the spot, his body trembles like an aspen leaf. He can barely breathe, still doesn't dare open his eyes.

Peter leans his forehead against his. "I love you, Tim. This doesn't change anything. At best, it will make me a better partner for you and a good ally for the ace community."

Tim breathes out a ragged breath. "You're not mad?"

"I am upset. But I understand that keeping this to yourself

must have been hard for you. We'll have to talk. A lot. But you're worth it, Tim. Always was, and always will be." He brushes away the tears rolling down Tim's cheeks. "You'll never have to hide from me."

"Anne, she..."

"...regrets that she was stupid enough to let you go. Of course, if you want to go back to her..."

Tim interrupts him with a kiss. He hopes it says what his mouth can't form words for. He puts all his love in it, all longings that only Peter can sate, all his wishes for a future together.

There will be fences to mend, texts with apologies and explanations to send. But they can wait. Now, Tim needs to feel that he and Peter are truly good.

Tim pushes a hand under Peter's shirt, caresses the skin there. "I want to feel you, Pete. Please."

"Tim. You don't have to."

"But I need you. I need to feel you, babe."

Peter nods in understanding. "Let's go get our Sunday cuddles."

"Yes," Tim chuckles. "Yes."

PURPLE

Chris knocks at his big sister's door. She calls him in, her room mostly dipped in darkness save for the dressing table she cajoled their parents into buying for her 17th birthday.

She turns to Chris with a bright smile. Her sibling parts his lips but the sight of her leaves him speechless.

"You need something?" Beatrice asks, arching a perfectly styled eyebrow.

"I..." Chris tries. "I forgot why I came here," he says, his heart beating a little faster. He racks his brain. "Oh, right. I wanted to ask if you could drive me to the mall tomorrow. Dad said we can have the car, but Mum's working the afternoon shift, so..."

"Are you going on a date?" Beatrice asks, a teasing tone lacing the words.

Chris rolls his eyes. "No, I'm just hanging out with my mates."

"I've got football training until two, but afterwards, why not? I meant to do some shopping anyway."

She turns back to the mirror and grabs a pair of fake lashes. She glances at Chris' reflection. "Anything else?"

Chris chews his lip. "Can... can I watch you doing your make-up?"

Beatrice stops still, the tweezers with the glued lashes hanging mid-air. "Um... if you want to." She furrows her brow for a short moment, then resumes putting the lashes onto her real ones.

Chris sits down on the edge of her bed and watches her

every move.

"You're always beautiful, but today you look even better," Chris says, hoping that the fairy lights surrounding him don't give away the blush that creeps into his cheeks.

They've always been close, but looking at her, this is more than just siblings sharing a space. He doesn't understand it himself. Sometimes, he wants to be like Beatrice, beautifully dressed and dolled up. But that's not what boys should want. It's just... today, Chris doesn't feel much like a boy.

"Are you alright?" Beatrice asks, and Chris only realises now that the loud sigh he heard came out of his own mouth.

"Yes. Why wouldn't I be?"

Beatrice's brows state clearly that she doesn't believe him.

"What's going on, Chrissie?" she asks, a hint of concern tinting her voice. She barely calls him by his childhood name nowadays, but it feels good to hear it. It seems more fitting somehow.

"I don't know. I'm... I just love your make-up. I wish I could do that, too," Chris presses out. He fidgets with the comforter and runs his fingers over the seams. He doesn't dare look at her.

Silence falls between them, and when it grows too heavy, he looks up at his frowning sister.

"Forget what I said," he says hastily and gets up from the bed.

"I could show you," Beatrice offers. "You have a lovely face as is but I think I could... you know," she says and wiggles her fingers before her face, her lips curving into a soft smile.

Chris' face breaks out into a grin. "You would?"

"Sure. Just let me quickly fix my make-up. You can choose a colour for your eye shadow while I'm on it."

She pushes her eye shadow palette into Chris' hand and returns her gaze to the mirror.

"I think the purples would make your eyes pop," she says.

"Purple?" Chris asks, a sudden swell of fear and excitement battling in his chest.

"We can go with nudes if you want something simpler," Beatrice says, glancing at him.

"No, purple sounds great," Chris mumbles. A smile tugs on the corners of his lips. He always liked the colour, but boys' clothes turn pretty boring when you hit puberty. And it's not that he likes pulling attention to himself at school. He prefers to blend in, to hide himself from sight in oversized jumpers and other baggy clothes. But that doesn't mean he doesn't envy his sister sometimes for being allowed to wear all these colourful, glittery, stunning shirts and dresses.

It's not that he doesn't like his wardrobe. He really does, most days. It's rather confusing, if he's absolutely honest. But maybe that's normal. Not that he could ask his mates about it.

He watches Beatrice setting her make-up with a spray that smells faintly like lavender.

"You're so pretty," he exclaims, and Beatrice chuckles.

"Thanks. I'm glad I got mum's cheekbones."

Chris' smile falters a little. "Yeah, mine are probably unsalvageable."

Beatrice clicks her tongue. "That's nonsense, Chrissie, and you know it. You look good."

"For a boy, you mean."

"Well, you *are* a boy." She shrugs, but her gaze lingers on Chris' face in a way that likely has nothing to do with figuring out what technique might accentuate his face. "You know I'll always love you, right?" she asks after a long moment of silence. The question makes Chris squirm. He doesn't even know why.

"Sure. Whatever."

Beatrice chuckles. "Okay. Let's start. First things first. I'll clean your face, and then we'll use a primer."

Chris looks shyly at his sister as she runs a cleaning pad over his face. This is nothing a boy should do. Why does it feel so good then?

"Oh, I know what I'm gonna do," Beatrice exclaims and taps on her phone. "This guy I'm watching on YouTube has a face similar to yours. His creations are incredible!"

Chris furrows his brow. A guy doing make-up? Chris squirms on the mattress.

Beatrice turns the screen to her sibling. Chris' mouth falls open. This man is beautiful.

"I could never look like that."

Beatrice rolls her eyes. "I'll prove you wrong," she smirks and gets to work. Chris feels his heart speeding up, nearly beating out of his chest. What if it looks terrible? Or even worse, what if he likes it?

"Hey, breathe, bro. I'm not gonna hurt you," Beatrice cackles.

"Sorry, it's just..."

Her hand holding the brush falls to her thigh. "Exciting?" she offers. Chris nods. "I felt the same the first time I wore mascara. Like a passage to being a woman or something. Mum put it on. I looked terrible because I cried so much." She laughs. "But Mum fixed it with a million cotton buds."

"You won't laugh if I cry?"

"Everyone cries in the beginning, Chrissie. It's part of it.

You're gonna look beautiful when I'm done with you." They share a smile, but the tender moment breaks when the doorbell rings. Chris freezes. He's not expecting anyone.

"Oh, that's Marie," Beatrice says.

Chris relaxes somewhat. "She's here to pick you up," he states.

"We wanted to chat a little before we drive over to the party. Is that okay? She's a big fan," Beatrice says, pointing at the screen of her phone.

"O-okay."

Chris pinches the flesh between his thumb and his pointer, trying hard to calm his racing heart. The spot is angry red when the girls enter the room.

"Oh, Chris. This looks awesome," Marie exclaims.

"You think?" he asks, glancing at Beatrice who probably prepared her on their way up if Marie's easy acceptance is anything to go by. Gone is the time when she liked to tease him for his sloppy looks.

"You totally rock that colour."

Chris smiles shyly at her.

"What do you think? Purple lipstick?" Beatrice asks her friend.

"A dark one, yes. His eyes are so pretty, the lips shouldn't pull the attention away," Marie replies.

Butterflies storm through Chris' stomach. No one has ever called him pretty before. It feels good.

Beatrice keeps on working, discussing techniques and materials with Marie, a conversation that totally goes over Chris' head. But he imagines what he might look like in the end. It makes him feel giddy with anticipation.

"Don't smile so much," Beatrice scolds him half-heartedly. "Or else I'll never get this contour right."

"Sorry," he says. He has no idea what a contour is, but it must be something important, so he tries his best to keep his face muscles relaxed.

It takes a while longer until Beatrice asks him to close his eyes and hold his breath, lavender engulfing him with the spray setting his make-up.

He still doesn't breathe when Beatrice beckons him to her dressing table.

"Give me a sec," he croaks, trying his best to make his lungs draw air. He chuckles nervously. The moment of truth has come.

She squeezes his hand. "You look fabulous."

"Yes. You're beautiful, Chris," Marie agrees. "You can totally pull off this look."

Chris smiles at them a little strained before he pushes off the bed and takes a look in the mirror. His hand goes to his cheek of its own accord, his lips parting in surprise. He slumps into the chair, studies every line and every angle.

"This is..." Chris has no words for what he sees in the mirror, the part of him he always knew existed but never dared to let see the light of day.

Beatrice smirks at him. "Done by a genius."

Chris elbows her softly, but secretly, he agrees. He looks way closer to how he feels today than he did an hour ago. It seems a bit much, somehow strange, but also familiar. This is him. At least in part.

"Doesn't match your hoodie, though," Marie points out.

Chris shrugs. "No one will see it anyway." It's a shame,

really, but probably for the better.

"But I'd like to put you on Insta," Beatrice says. "Only if you agree, of course."

Chris worries his lip, letting go of it when he realises he might mess up the lipstick that he really likes.

"Do you think anyone will realise it's me?"

Beatrice shakes her head. "Not if I don't tag you."

Chris smiles. "What should I wear?" he asks after a long moment of consideration.

"What about Bea's grey shirt with the sequins?" Marie suggests.

A minute later, Chris has changed in more ways than just his clothes. The shirt hugs him in all the right places, is soft and girly, makes him feel good in his skin.

The girls style his hair, and to his surprise, Chris likes himself in the pictures his sister is taking, even those without the filters.

"Thanks, Bee," he says after she sent him the pics. "How do I take it off again?" he asks.

"You wanna get rid of it already?"

Chris shakes his head. "Not really. But it's a bit much for an evening of gaming."

"Then come to the party with us. It's gonna be fun," Beatrice says.

Chris quirks a wry smile. "Don't wanna embarrass you in front of your friends."

Beatrice rolls her eyes. "You will if you keep on saying stupid shit like that. It's pretty chill. You may actually like my friends."

"But I'm..." he waves his hand awkwardly in front of his

body.
	"Whoever you wanna be, Chrissie."
	And that she is. At least for tonight.

82

REFUGE

Simon lets his gaze wander over the people in the café from his usual spot in the booth furthest away from the entrance. He's been struggling with the last paragraph for at least twenty minutes now, and sometimes, it helps when he emerges from the fictional world he's building to the harshness and beauty of reality to find a new angle or an idea that refuses to come otherwise.

Su, the owner, is serving the bar as she usually does on weekdays. He can see a few familiar faces scattered around the café—the person with the rainbow-coloured hair that always hides their face as they grip their mug so tightly that the knuckles turn white; the mother with a sleeping baby in her wrap nursing their usual chai latte; a man named Jona who he'd shared his table with during the last pride parade when the café was surprisingly crammed full at 2pm and Simon's book deadline collided with his neighbour's refurbishing plans.

There are many new faces, too, and Simon watches them with as little intrusion as possible. People watching is one of his favourite pastimes, but he knows it can turn creepy, and he really doesn't want anyone to feel uncomfortable, just because he's a curious fella.

Su smiles at him when she catches him looking, and he raises his empty mug, knowing already that it's a bad idea to put even more caffeine into his system. But as much as he loves this little space, filled with acceptance, the smell of freshly baked scones, and a bouquet of people that never grows boring—as mundane and normal-as-it-gets as it might be at most times—their choice of caffeine-free coffee is the worst in town. And Simon really doesn't like any other concoctions they're offering but the black coffee that Su fills into his mug with a gentle smile curving her lips.

"How's it going?" she asks, nodding at his laptop.

Simon scrunches his nose.

"I managed a hundred words or so, and I think I'll delete all of them."

She gives him a sympathetic smile.

"It'll come to you, sweetheart. No worries."

Simon quirks a smile and lets his head fall back against the headrest of the bench.

"From your mouth to God's ears!"

He watches her return to the bar and cracks his neck. He marks the paragraph and presses the return key.

'Let's try this again,' he thinks and hits the keyboard. The words come easier this time, the vision of the scene clearer, now that he's emptied his mind for a moment.

Time flies by. The ringing of the bell over the entrance doesn't pull him out of his writing daze anymore. His coffee grows cold, but he couldn't care less. He's fully in his own world now, and he stops checking the word count, just goes with the flow.

Until someone slides into his booth, that is.

Simon looks up from his laptop and around the café. Many tables are empty, and the man opposite him is way too young to flirt with him. Besides, he really doesn't want to. He's here to work.

"Can I do something for you?" Simon asks, because he was raised to be polite, and in all honesty, he's highly confused by the worried Bambi eyes staring at him.

Maybe it's a fan? It's a possibility. He did readings in the café before, and while his novels are more catered to an adult audience, they are loved by some adolescents as well. He's a bit annoyed by the boy disturbing his workflow, but he isn't an arsehole. It's not as if he has never stepped over other people's boundaries involuntarily.

The young man blushes fiercely, his eyes darting to the bar. Simon follows his spooked gaze. Only one customer is leaning against it, brazenly staring down the teen opposite him.

Unease spreads in Simon's stomach.

"Is everything okay?" he asks, concern lacing his words.

The young man turns his eyes back to him and leans forward, propping up his forearms on the table.

"He's been following me for at least thirty minutes now. I can't shake him," he whispers. "I know I'm just a stranger, but could you pretend to be my older brother or something?"

Simon blinks at him. He has never been a good actor, but he has met his fair share of unwanted advances and creepy followers to know how much it can freak one out.

"I've got you," he says. "Is it okay if I touch your arm?"

The stranger nods.

Simon reaches out and circles his biceps.

"I'm Simon. What's your name?"

The boy looks around before he whispers, "Dawid."

Simon smiles.

"Well, hello, Dawid. Nice to meet you. I'll go to the bar now. If anyone asks, it's your birthday, okay?"

Dawid looks slightly confused but he nods anyway.

Simon slides off the bench and walks to Su, leaning against

the bar directly next to the creepy guy.

"Su, darling, could I have some of your Sacher torte? It's my little brother's birthday, and our mother's oven conked out. Can't leave him without a birthday cake, can I?"

The café owner furrows her brow. They've been friends long enough for her to know that he's an only child. Simon tries to put as much sincerity into his gaze as possible to make her understand. And she does.

"I bet he wants it with a hot chocolate with cream," she says.

"You know him too well," Simon chuckles. It sounds pretty convincing. Maybe it's the relief that he isn't called out on his mediocre acting.

He turns away and watches Dawid fidgeting with a paper napkin. The boy truly looks like a deer caught in the headlights. Poor guy.

"I'll bring your order to the table. Anything for you?" Su asks.

"A slice of apple pie and… a glass of lemonade," he says. "My heart is putting any racehorse to shame," he chuckles.

Su smirks at him.

"Gotcha, Si."

Simon nods and returns to his table. He closes his laptop and puts it into his bag. He'll wait for this creep to leave, will escort the boy home if need be.

"I hope you like Sacher cake," he says. "And hot chocolate?"

Dawid smiles for the first time since he sat down at the table.

"I could do with some sugar, I guess."

"You don't need to eat it," Simon makes clear.

"I'll pay for it," Dawid says.

"On your birthday?" Simon asks especially loud. "Do you want to shame your big brother?"

Dawid snickers, and the tension in Simon's body subsides a little.

"Tell me about you. Can be true or totally made up," Simon prompts.

Dawid laughs.

"I'm finishing High School next summer, will go to Community College."

"What degree?"

Dawid shrugs.

"I want art, but my parents think I should do business or accounting."

Simon breathes a sigh. He had that same discussion with his parents a decade ago.

"As your temporary big brother, let me tell you—do what you want to. College is hard enough without forcing yourself with a topic you don't have a real interest in."

Dawid smiles and glances at the bar. His shoulders relax minutely. Simon looks up just in time to see the creep beat a retreat.

He chuckles in relief.

Su brings his order and crumbles the receipt in her hand.

"On the house," she says, adding louder, "Happy birthday, Marcus."

Simon huffs a laugh. "The creep is gone. But thanks for playing along, Su."

She breathes out audibly and smiles at Dawid.

"Sorry that I didn't catch on to that. Just for future

reference—many cafés and bars help you to get out of a tricky situation if you ask for Angela or pretty much anybody. We usually understand that you need to get out of an uncomfortable date or something."

Dawid nods.

"Thanks, Su. Good to know."

"My pleasure," she replies. "Anything else I can get you?"

Both men shake their heads.

"I can eat this somewhere else," Dawid offers. "I don't want to bother you any longer."

Simon waves him off.

"You can stay as long as you want. And I can walk a bit of your way, if you wanna make sure he isn't waiting outside."

Dawid looks through the front windows.

"That would be cool. Thanks. For everything."

"It's nothing."

Dawid huffs a laugh and fills his mouth with cake.

"It was the truth, you know. I want to study art history and literature."

Simon leans forward.

"Sounds like a great combination. One best discussed over Sacher torte and apple pie."

Simon smirks, and Dawid leans back in his seat.

"You have no idea what you've gotten yourself into, *brother.*"

Simon laughs out loud.

"Let's see if I can top your enthusiasm for literature, shall we?"

CHICKEN SOUP

Amal slumps their back against the inside of their front door and lets out a long-drawn breath that might or might not be a sigh. The back of their head thumps thrice against the sturdy wood before they peel themself off it and kick their shoes away. Let future Amal take care of them.

They shuffle into the living room and face-plant into the sofa cushions. Everything hurts—every bone, every muscle, even the tip of their nose. Still, they went to work this morning. They doubt they will move until Monday. But thank Allah, it's Friday. No one needs them alive for the next two days.

Amal falls into a fitful sleep only seconds after this thought, getting rid of their day clothes bit by bit as their temperature rises. The socks go last, and the next time they awake, they pull the blanket over themself that their friend Susie crocheted. They pull the yellow corner to their face and nuzzle into the soft wool.

They wish she was here. Then, they needn't think about how to get water from the sink. Then they wouldn't need to take care of themself.

Usually, Amal loves living alone. There's nothing better than binge-watching a show without side-commentaries or flatmates who make them watch telly with headphones on. No one will curse over the discarded shoes on the floor or yesterday's dishes piled up on the kitchen worktop and the unfolded laundry on their bed.

But right now, it would be awesome to have someone to fold, do the washing-up, and boil the kettle for some tea. Their throat is really dry but they can't make themself get up.

Amal slides back into sleep, dreaming bewildering things. Work buddies are sitting at their kitchen table, their mother critiques their work in front of their boss, which makes even less sense than them inviting their colleagues over.

They kick off the blanket, their boxers and tanktop drenched in sweat. They sleep another round, pull the blanket back over themself as they wake, then kick them off again. There's simply no right way of doing this.

They get up from the couch on wobbly legs and sway more than walk to the kitchen. Waiting for the kettle isn't an option, so they grab the biggest water bottle in their fridge and schlep it back to the sofa.

The cold water burns in their throat, and after a few painful gulps, they sink back on the couch and into sleep again. Hydration is absolutely overrated.

Amal wakes up from clattering in their kitchen. But that can't be real. They are living alone.

'A dream in a dream. Brilliant,' they think. Exhaustion claims every part of their body, muscles sore as if they had run a marathon. Their eyes fall on the coffee table, where the nearly empty water bottle stands, cap screwed close. When did they drink? And how the heck did they manage to close the bottle with their fingers feeling like hotdogs, wobbly and swollen?

Yeah. Most definitely a dream.

Amal turns with a groan, their head pounding to the beat of their heart. Being sick is bad enough, but dreaming of being sick *while* being sick is just the cherry on top of the cake.

They close their eyes and try to catch another dream. There must be better ones available.

"Open your eyes, sweetheart. Let's get you cleaned up," a gentle voice wakes them.

Amal furrows their brow. It's dark around them save the light falling in from the hallway.

"Aaron," they ask, "whatcha doin' here?"

Aaron chuckles. "Taking care of you, silly." He sounds as if it were the most logical thing. Maybe it is. Amal can't really find a reason why not. He's their best friend, after all. He has never seen them sick before, though.

"How did you know?" Amal asks and allows him to pull them up into a sitting position.

"You didn't turn up to movie night, so I checked in on you," Aaron says. No, that can't be right. Movie night is Saturday. They just came home from work.

"Ronny, I..." they trail off, the world turning way too fast for their liking.

"You need a bath, fresh clothes and liquids," he decides. All of that sounds amazing, to be honest. But it also sounds unachievable.

"Ron, I can't..."

"Do you want to, sweetheart?"

Amal would shake their head if they didn't fear to topple over from it.

Aaron opens the bottle and holds it to their lips. They take a sip and shake their head. The water settles like freezing lead in their stomach.

"Okay, that was a flop. You definitely need soup. And maybe a bath is a bit much, huh, Ams?"

They nod.

"Okay. Plan B," Aaron says and disappears.

Amal hears him rummaging around their flat. They don't mind. What could be worse than seeing them in this state?

Aaron returns with short pyjamas, a washcloth, and a bowl filled with water. He sits down on the coffee table and takes their hand before he runs the damp cloth over the heated skin of their arms. He washes them gently. Amal breathes a sigh. This feels good.

When he has washed every uncovered part of their body, he puts the cloth back into the bowl and leaves Amal to do the rest.

"Are you done?" Aaron calls from the kitchen after giving them a few minutes.

"Mmh," Amal hums and pushes themself up on wobbly feet.

"Uh-uh. You sit down and eat your soup," comes from the door.

"Ron."

"No, I don't accept arguments."

"You sound like your mother," Amal groans.

Aaron chuckles. "I won't deny that. She wishes you a speedy recovery."

Amal breathes a sigh. "You told your mother?" He nods as he places a bowl of hot soup on the coffee table. "That means she'll tell mine. Aaron," they whine.

"She won't come. I promised her to take care of you. I know how overbearing she can be."

Amal sinks back into the sofa cushion. "Thank you."

"You're welcome. Now, eat my bubbie's chicken soup so that you regain your strength. *Bessie* is waiting for us," Aaron says and tucks them in. Amal closes their eyes for a long moment before they take the bowl from Aaron's hand, a small smile playing on their lips.

Yes, being sick sucks. But here, on this couch, with Bubbie Rivka's soup slowly filling their stomach and Aaron setting up the TV, life sucks a little less.

A RAINY NIGHT

Agnes has always liked the rain. Thunderstorms were her favourites. While her older brother had always hidden under his blanket, hands tightly pressed over his ears, she had opened the window, breathing in the rain's scent, feeling the electricity in the air, the hairs on her arms standing up in fearful delight. She was the one who her mother scolded not to dance in the rain, not to collect the sky's drops in her mouth and *behave*. Who she caught dressed in only her Spiderman pyjamas and wellies, jumping through the puddles, thanking the rain god with her dance.

There was a special kind of muttering her mother had reserved for Agnes' rain antics, one that held all her disdain and lack of understanding. Her father on the other hand understood Agnes perfectly. He always took her on weekend trips, especially when the forecast had promised rain, their waxed jackets and hats fixed staples in their travel wardrobe. He still sends her updates from his weather station that he bought after retirement, the precipitation always on top of the list.

Rain has never lost its fascination, never fails to revive Agnes's spirits and make her feel one with nature and the universe. And so she finds herself on the porch at the back of her flat, safe from the pouring rain that is rushing to the ground, its white noise stealing any other sound.

She's wrapped in a fluffy blanket, woollen socks warming her feet that she keeps tucked under her body. Her hands are warmed by a cup of tea and the dash of her favourite whiskey infusing it. Lightning strikes in the distance, the following thunder rolling over her skin like a physical force. She needed that today, even more than sleep.

Agnes lets her head fall back against the wooden panelling of the wall and closes her eyes, the scent of rain flooding her senses. She can pretend she's eight again, the wind tugging on the flimsy fabric of her pyjamas and her body resilient enough to risk getting soaked wet, returning home with blue lips frozen into a wide grin. She can't risk that anymore, but she can still smell the rain, and she does whenever the opportunity arises. No one and nothing will take this away from her, ever.

Agnes startles when a hand cups her shoulder, the gentle touch ripping through her like a thunderbolt.

"Jesus! Tammy!" Agnes chuckles. "You scared me."

"Sorry," her flatmate says. "Didn't mean to."

"Why are you up?" Agnes asks. Tammy gestures to the outside world. Agnes nods. "Same. Wanna share a Hot Toddy with me?"

"I may as well," Tammy says and fills a mug with the still hot liquid pouring out of the thermos. She takes a sip and arches an eyebrow. "It's strong," she comments.

"Don't need to get up tomorrow," Agnes says and tightens the blanket around her shoulders.

"I have the afternoon shift," Tammy says. "Want me to get anything from the store?"

"Nah. I've got a delivery lined up. But thanks." Agnes smiles a little strained. She doesn't want Tammy to play her caregiver. They're flatmates, friends. When it gets to the point where she'll need assistance, she'll hire a nurse or domestic help. She's always been independent, she won't give that up now.

She knows, everyone just wants to help, but she's fine. She

can still manage her life, can still enjoy things, and she can do her friggin' grocery shopping, thank you very much.

Agnes takes a deep breath. Her anger follows every beautiful gesture like the thunder follows a lightning flash. She's working on it, but it's hard sometimes. She didn't live her life to the fullest and now, every other week, she has to erase another item on her bucket list, never to be fulfilled. Eventually, it will be empty. This shouldn't be the case at her age. She feels betrayed, and she feels like a burden. It's simply too much sometimes.

"What's going on?" Tammy asks gently, looking out into the rain. Agnes glances at her and breathes a sigh.

"You still sure you wanna stay with little moody me?" she asks.

Tammy laughs out loud. "Oh, Agnes. There's no one I'd rather live with. You're more fun than you think."

Agnes quirks a lopsided smile. "I used to be fun."

Tammy shakes her head. "You still are. It's just a lot right now. It's fine. We'll get you to a new normal, and then, your beautiful smile will shine more often again."

Agnes picks at her blanket. "It's going to get worse, Tammy."

"It's going to be *different*. But I'm here, till the end of the line."

"Tammy."

"What? I told you, you're like a sister to me. And family sticks together, through thick and thin."

Agnes huffs a mirthless laugh. Tammy is kind enough not to call her out for it.

"Hey, it's gonna be alright. You'll see. After every rain, the sun returns. You know that."

"I always loved the rain," Agnes says.

"Because it clears the air?"

Agnes shakes her head. No, it's not that. It felt endless, calm, the world coming to a halt. Maybe that's why she's stuck in her head, she muses. She always dreaded the sun and the business returning with it. The rain felt safe, and maybe, this unclear in-between feels safer, too. It's likely a shaky analogy, but Tammy is right. There is a place beyond the rain, beyond feeling stuck. Maybe this episode of her life is meant to clear her, to let go of what she carried for too long and find what she truly needs. It's shit, but it is what it is.

"Maybe I should walk the Camino de Santiago, as long as I still can," she says.

"That Spanish pilgrims' way? You're an atheist, sweetheart."

Agnes chuckles. "Some places are still holy."

Tammy nods, understanding her as usual. Agnes stretches out her hand and squeezes hers.

"Could you bring me cheesecake from the bakery down at the river?" she asks. Tammy smiles.

"Sure."

They sit in silence for a while longer, Tammy's head leaning on Agnes' shoulder, until the rain drizzles out and the rays of the morning sun break through the grey clouds.

The Hot Toddy is cold by now, but Agnes feels warm inside, revived and – despite the lack of sleep – full of energy, ready to take on whatever will come. Agnes loves the rain, but maybe, she can learn to love the after, too.

SILLY, LITTLE DORKS

Oscar looks at the messenger icon floating on his screen. It's been years since he's seen Zarah. They used to be best friends in college, but they lost sight of each other, with her moving to a different part of the country and all that.

He barely uses the app anymore, only stays there for the groups that he can't let go of. Even his username is still his high school nickname, and there's not a single photo on his timeline that shows himself. Oscar's finger hovers over the display, his stomach tying into knots.

'Ah, fuck it!' he thinks. What does he have to lose?

He opens the app and smiles at the profile picture welcoming him. Zarah sports a wedding gown and the brightest smile Oscar has ever seen on her. She's radiant and looks so happy, it aches that he hadn't been there to catch this moment with his own eyes.

Her message reads, *Hey, hun. Moved back to town. Wanna get a coffee sometime and reminisce about when we were young and free? XX*

Oscar smiles at the message. Short as they always used to be, right to the point. Zarah can be a chatterbox in person, but that never translated to text messages. She seems to want to rekindle their friendship. Oscar is elated and freaked out in equal measures.

He taps the reply box and stares at the keyboard. So much has happened in the last decade, and she doesn't know anything about it. Should he just dump it into the chat and hope for the best? Should he tell her in person?

He hates this. He's come out so often before, and every frigging time, it's nerve-wracking all over again. He doesn't know how others do it. One might think you get used to it over time, but Oscar still hasn't.

The last time had been a while ago, though, with his world-travelling auntie. He barely crosses paths with people from his past anymore, though, and new acquaintances he usually doesn't tell. Why would he? It's not anybody's business.

But he and Zarah were so close, used to share a dorm room and all their secrets. It would be a shame not to meet if she's in the area. He'd love to show her what he created, who he's become. And he wants to know her joys, fuck-ups and successes, too, wants to find out if they still click as they did on that first day of college, when he entered their room, and she smirked at him, lying on her bed, Nirvana blaring from her tinny loudspeakers.

Hey, Zarah, he writes back. *Would love to catch up with you. A few things have changed on my side. Hope you're up for it.*

As soon as he's sent the message, the info that Zarah is typing appears. Oscar's stomach ties into knots. He takes deep breaths. There's no use in letting the anxiety curling in his chest wash all over his body. It's gonna be alright, no matter which way this goes.

Oh, I can't wait to hear everything about it. Is the old cat café still open?

Oscar laughs out loud. He can't believe she still remembers the place. But why wouldn't she? They basically lived in it for years, pet therapy included.

Yeah. No cats anymore, but they have great muffins now.

Mmm. Awesome, Zarah replies. *When are you free? Now, by*

any chance?

Oscar looks at the clock. He meant to pick up candles for the shop, but that can wait. He's far too pent up to wait another day to meet his old friend.

I could be there in thirty minutes, Oscar writes. Better get this over with.

Great. See you. XX

Oscar enters the café with a weird mix of knots and butterflies filling his stomach. He waves over to Mimi behind the counter, then scans the well-filled tables in the room lined with bookshelves. He can see Zahra's page-boy haircut from afar. He smiles at her, but she looks right past him. He doesn't blame her. She's expecting someone looking way different to him.

He walks over to her table – *their* table, all those years ago – and stops, smiling at her shyly. She looks up from the menu, a tiny frown on her forehead. Still, she smiles.

"I'm not ready to order. I'm waiting for a friend," she says.

Oscar chuckles nervously.

"I'm not the waiter," he says. "I'm the friend you're waiting for."

She stares at him for a long, long moment before realisation spreads over her features and her lips part in surprise.

"Oh," she finally says. Oscar worries the inside of his cheek. "Now I know what you meant by 'things have changed'," Zarah chuckles. "You were always good looking, but *man!*" She whistles.

Oscar laughs out loud, the relief washing through him

making him a little dizzy for a second. "You nearly got it right," he says and hovers awkwardly next to the table before he sits down. She manoeuvres her wheelchair a little.

"What? No hug? What kind of a reunion is that?" she smirks, and Oscar would swear that she hasn't aged a single day since the last time they met. She still has the same shining, mischievous eyes, the easy smile, and a laugh as clear as a bell.

They hug for a long moment, the embrace familiar and new all at once.

"How have you been?" Oscar asks when she finally lets go of him. He glances at the wheelchair. That one is new.

"Good. Married last summer."

Oscar nods. He got the hint.

"Congratulations! Do you have pictures of your spouse?"

Zarah's eyes light up.

"Yes," she says and pulls out her phone. "I met Ed during rehab. He's the best."

They look at pictures for a while. Oscar can't stop grinning. There she is—travelling to Paris, kissing her husband under a mistletoe, giving a TED talk... One photo shows her and Ed at a convention in a Leia/Han cosplay. They reminisce about the Halloween party to which they went as Harley Quinn and Poison Ivy. Everyone mistook them for a couple. Good old times.

"Got anyone special in your life?" Zarah asks after putting her phone down.

"Oh, plenty," Oscar chuckles. He fidgets with the candle holder on the table for a moment before he adds, "A dog, two cats, and a rescued hare living in my garden. But romance isn't really my thing if you were thinking about that."

"That's cool," Zarah says without missing a beat. "You always wanted to have pets. I'm so happy you can have them now. What else are you up to?"

Oscar smiles and extends his arms, looking around the café.

"I own this place," he says and enjoys the surprise washing over Zarah's face. She slaps his shoulder playfully.

"You're kidding me!"

"No," Oscar chuckles. "I wrote half of my dissertation over there in the corner because my flatmate was... let's settle on 'special'. I sat here for hours over a single mug of coffee, and Elli didn't say a single word about it."

"She always had a heart of gold."

"She really did. One day, she told me she had to close the café because of her age. I was heartbroken. I mean, this was an institution."

Zarah nods.

"It would have been a shame to let it turn into a coffee shop from one of those big chains or something."

"Absolutely!"

"And you bought it? Just like that?"

Oscar chuckles.

"No, not on a whim. I'm too organised for that. I had planned to open a bookshop, had everything ready to start as soon as I had my doctorate. I just needed to rework the plan a little, worked here for three months to learn the ropes, et voilà!"

Zarah shakes her head and smiles. "It sounds like a dream come true."

Oscar runs his hand through his hair and nods.

"It truly is."

"I miss the cats, though," she says, pursing her lips to a pout as she looks around.

"Yeah. But they still keep Elli company. Do you want to drink something?" Oscar asks. "I guess my employee doesn't want to impose."

"Yes. And something to eat. I skipped lunch."

"What do you want?"

" Surprise me." Zarah grins.

"I think I can do that," he replies and walks to the counter. He's confident that she'll love their mochaccino. He smiles at Mimi as he prepares two of them.

"Everything alright, boss?" she asks.

"Everything's perfect," he says and grins over at Zarah. She waves at him, just like the silly little dork she once was, and fully the grown-up she's become. He waves back and grins to himself. She probably thought just the same about him this very second.

SHAVE IT OFF

"Dad?" Victor calls from upstairs, his voice cracking. His father Ben puts the book he's reading in the living room down on his lap and calls back, "What?"

"Can you come and help me?"

Ben breathes a sigh and marks the page. He can't remember the last time he managed to read a full chapter in one go with a twelve and a sixteen-year-old in the house. But truth be told, he wouldn't want it any other way. Well, most of the time.

He walks up the stairs, his bare feet sinking into the new carpet he put down a week ago. He smiles at the green and blue tartan. It was the right choice. His partner Rosella most definitely has a nose for interior design.

Ben looks into his son's room but finds it empty.

"Where are you, Vic?" he calls.

"In the bathroom."

Ben furrows his brow. What has he done in there to need his help? Hopefully not another emergency requiring a plunger.

To his surprise, Ben finds his firstborn with his back to the double sink, no apparent flooding in sight. Victor shifts his weight nervously from one foot to the other, though, hiding something behind his back. Ben takes a deep breath in preparation and asks, "What happened?"

"Nothing," Victor smirks. "I just thought... I wanted to shave and..." He grins as he presents a razor and a can of shaving foam.

Ben's heart leaps in his chest. He has been waiting for this day for quite some time, but Victor loved his first moustache so much that Ben slowly started believing he would never have the pleasure of teaching his son this skill before Victor would move out to college.

"You wanna get rid of your beard?" Ben asks smiling.

Victor shrugs his shoulders. "Minnie says it tickles too much when we're kissing," he says, a blush quickly spreading from his neck to his cheeks.

"Your mom doesn't like it, either," Ben chuckles.

"Is that why you have a goatee?"

"Partly. But I think it suits me, don't you think?"

Victor nods. "I hope I'll be able to have one, one day."

Ben smiles. "Mine didn't grow over night, either. So, what is your plan? All clean shave?"

"Yeah. The sides are still patchy anyway."

"Alright. Show me what you got?"

Victor hands his father the can and the razor.

"You shouldn't have spent money on that," Ben says, checking the home brand of their local supermarket. "This razor will likely irritate your skin. The foam is alright, but when it's empty, I'd suggest switching to shaving cream. It has fewer ingredients, produces less rubbish, and you can use it with a shaving brush."

Victor's face falls a little, and Ben reprimands himself inwardly. He didn't mean to belittle his son's choices. It must have been such a great moment to buy them. At least, that's what it was like for him.

"But I can show you both techniques," he adds. "Shaving foam has its benefits, too. Do you still have the receipt?" Victor nods, smiling a little again. "Then let's return the razor. I bought you one for sensitive skin a while ago. Didn't want you to make the same mistakes I did with my first shaves."

Victor chuckles. "Did no one teach you?"

Ben shakes his head. "You know, your granda needed a bit of time to come around to the thought of having another son, and your uncle lived abroad at that time. I felt silly asking him about it over the phone and tried it on my own."

Victor makes a face. "It didn't go well, I assume."

"Nah. I made all the classical beginners' mistakes," Ben says and rummages through the bathroom cabinet until he finds the razor in the back of it. "Here we go. Did you already give yourself a catlick?"

Victor shakes his head.

"Okay. Wash your face and neck with hot water and pat it dry. I could do with a shave, too. Let's do it together."

They wash themselves at the double basin, grinning at each other in the mirror.

"It's important that you always wash your face beforehand," Ben explains. "Otherwise, it's more likely that you'll cut yourself and hairs grow in, which isn't fun. I usually do it right after a shower. Then you either put the foam from your can in your hand and put it right on your skin *or* you do it like me and foam up the cream or the shaving soap with a brush. I prefer the latter, though hands are just fine."

Ben demonstrates his routine, and Victor watches him with wide, curious eyes. Ben stifles a chuckle. It's lovely to see his son grow into a man, his body that looks nearly adult now while his mind is still sometimes as playful as that of a child. He hopes he'll keep that for a while or – even better – will never lose it. Adulthood is hard enough as it is. He remembers well the big changes he went through during his first puberty and the more rapid ones when he started testosterone. He savoured his first facial hair just as much as his oldest does. It's probably a man thing, Ben ponders.

He moves the shaving brush in circles over his skin, a familiar movement by now that he doesn't even have to think about anymore. But he still remembers the thrill of that first time, too, the tangy scent of the shaving soap he had used back then, the sting of the aftershave that had way too much alcohol in it. Victor will hopefully not have to walk into all the pits Ben fell into while figuring out how to do this right. There are enough other mistakes he can make that will form him into the man he'll become.

A smile tugs on Ben's lips when he explains to Victor how to move the shaver over his skin and the importance of cream right after cleaning off the last remnants of the foam. Victor beams at him and knocks their shoulders together in a silent thankyou.

"I'm glad I have a dad to show me the ropes," Victor says, smiling at his father in a way that makes him morph right back to the little boy who Ben could swear he and Rosella brought home just yesterday.

Ben beams right back at him. "I'm happy about that, too."

HOME WORK

"Thank you so much for coming home early, Eva," Mia says and presses a kiss to her sister's cheek. "I just don't know what to do with her today. Everything I say makes her explode."

Eva waves her off and shrugs out of her parka. "I get it. I couldn't stand it when Mum tried to help me with homework, either."

Mia chuckles and takes the jacket from her hands. "Yeah. I still remember your screaming contests. Though Sharon could give you a run for your money."

Eva squeezes Mia's shoulder. "It's a lot right now. Don't you worry. Everything's gonna be alright."

Mia nods. She probably knows that Eva doesn't only mean the maths homework of her fourth-grader.

"She's in the living room," she says and lets out a sigh.

"Take a break. I've got this," Eva reassures, and with a grateful nod, Mia leaves for the winter garden.

"Hey, pumpkin," Eva says as she enters the living room. Little Sharon looks up from her maths book, cheeks as red as her eyes, dried tear-tracks painting her skin. "Bad day?" her aunt asks and sits down next to her.

"Stupid maths," Sharon blurts out and pushes the book away.

"I get it," Eva says. "Numbers are so annoying. But we need them, pumpkin."

"I know," Sharon says with a long-suffering sigh. "But I'm too stupid for it."

Eva clicks her tongue. "You're the smartest kid I know," she protests.

"I'm the *only* kid you know."

Eva snickers. "True. But that makes you also my favourite, and I only keep company with the best, smartest, prettiest, funniest people on the planet."

That makes Sharon laugh.

"Show me what you got there," Eva asks and after a long moment of worrying her bottom lip, Sharon pushes the book over the table.

"Oh, that's cool stuff. Division is awesome," Eva exclaims. Her enthusiasm was probably a little over the top.

Sharon arches an eyebrow. There's no way to fool this girl, but Eva has known her since the day she was born, held Mia's hand during labour, was the one holding little Sharon against her chest while the midwife took care of her exhausted sister after 26 hours of birth. Sharon is smart, has a temper, and is the sweetest kid on earth. Eva does have comparisons, and – truth be told – she doesn't like most kids, but Sharon? Sharon is the exception to the rule. She'd do anything for the girl. That's why she proposed the two move in with her in their parents' house, after Mia's partner left her for another woman and the freedom of a childless life. It's not always easy, but it's nice to come home to freshly cooked meals and a new drawing waiting for her on the desk in her study every single day.

"You can divide things, right?" she asks, praying that her niece knows her multiplication tables.

Sharon rolls her eyes. "Of course. I learnt that in second grade." No kid her age should be able to sound this annoyed. Eva suppresses a laugh. That might not be helpful in the situation.

"Awesome. In that case, this will be easy as pie."

They get through the calculus slowly, but the more Sharon works out the more confident and faster she becomes.

"See? That wasn't too bad," Eva says and watches her niece happily putting her school stuff into her satchel. Sharon smiles, but she looks exhausted.

"Mummy was angry at me," she says quietly.

"I'm sure she wasn't, pumpkin. It's just a lot—the moving and the divorce. She wants to help you, but sometimes…"

Sharon nods. "Sometimes I get so angry, and then we're shouting."

"Yeah. Shouting is dumb, isn't it?"

"Yes."

"Maybe talk with your mum, now that you two are a bit calmer?" Eva suggests.

"Can we order pizza for tea?"

Eva smirks, "I need to talk to your mum about that."

Sharon rolls her eyes and hugs her aunt, already shouting for her mother. Eva's ears ring but she doesn't complain. She's just glad that she could help. Homework can be a melting point in the best of moments. She doesn't know how her sister manages it alone most of the time.

"I'm playing in the backyard!" Sharon yells after a short while and bangs the door shut behind her. Eva chuckles and walks to the winter garden where Mia is lying stretched out on the couch.

"You two good?" Eva asks. Mia bends her knees and Eva sits down in the free space that the movement created. She nudges her sister's leg and taps her thighs. Mia expands her legs with a sigh. She must have been on her feet all day.

"I think so. Thanks to you."

Eva shakes her head. "It's always better when the parent doesn't double as a teacher."

"What would I do without you?"

"You'd be the same badass mother as you are now."

Mia huffs a mirthless laugh.

"I mean it," Eva insists. Her sister accepts it in silence. "Mum said so, too," Eva adds.

"Did she? I wish she could tell me that to my face and not only to others behind my back."

Eva hums. It's how things usually go for Mia. Eva is their mother's favourite, and she isn't shy to share this truth in front of both her daughters and anyone else who's willing to listen to her praises about the successful businesswoman, free spirit, and independent person she is. Mia, on the other hand, only gets Eva's successes rubbed into her face, her own achievements belittled or ignored. Eva hates it, especially since she knows that Mia always dreamed about having a family. She doesn't deserve the malice. She deserves to hear with her own ears that she's doing great. But there's a snowball's chance in hell of that happening. Their mother's disappointment in her oldest will always win over empathy.

"But I guess I deserve that," Mia sighs. "I did what she warned me about: got married, had a child, then got discharged like a piece of crap. She predicted this would happen at my hen party."

"It could have played out differently, darling. Mum's not a psychic. She's still waiting for me to bring a partner home."

"She might get that, no? I thought your squish made you think about a QPR?" Mia asks.

Eva shrugs. "I'm not sure if he's partnership material. We'll see."

Mia nods. "Sharry asked for pizza?"

Eva chuckles. "Yeah. Okay with you?"

"Can I eat mine here on the sofa?" she asks chuckling.

"What about a pizza, telly, sofa night?" Eva suggests.

"Sounds perfect," Mia says and fishes for her phone. "*Antonio's* or *La Familia.*"

"Antonio's," Eva decides. "Their salami is better."

"Yes, ma'am."

They chuckle. Mia considers her sister for a long moment before saying, "If it's Sharon and I holding you back with Steve..."

Eva raises a hand. "Don't even finish that sentence. We're a package deal. The three musketeers."

"You don't have to put your life on hold for us, sis."

"I don't. Just because I contemplate a relationship for the first time in years doesn't mean it has precedence over what we have going on. Maybe he'll move in, maybe I'll move out, maybe everything stays the same. But one thing is clear: I will always be there for you and Sharon, no matter what."

Eva can see the tears collecting in her sister's eyes, and her heart grows heavy with emotions.

"Don't cry. You know I'll cry then, too," she pleads, already feeling the telltale prick in her eyes.

Mia chuckles and lets her head fall back on the armrest. "You're wonderful." She smiles.

"Wonderful enough to choose the movie?"

"Not sure about that," Mia muses with a fat smirk on her face, shoving her playfully. It's like they're teens again, the woman behind the grief shining through. Eva can't wait for the day when Mia will be over the pain and ready again to enjoy every minute of her life without a grey cloud hanging over her head. Until then, she'll just have to put in the work and provide a home for the three of them, whenever need be.

Don't miss out!

Visit the website below and you can sign up to receive emails whenever Liron A. Galston publishes a new book. There's no charge and no obligation.

https://books2read.com/r/B-A-CNSGF-IGIZB

BOOKS 2 READ

Connecting independent readers to independent writers.

About the Author

Liron writes short stories, flash fiction, and novels with queer characters taking the leading roles.

Grown up with mostly tragic queer storylines, they love writing stories that depict the real life of queer people.

They're married with children, are a passionate singer and love reading, binge-watching shows and all kinds of handcrafts.